ENEMY LINES

(NAVIGATOR SERIES BOOK ONE)

SD TANNER

Enemy Lines

Copyright © SD Tanner 2016

All rights reserved.

No part of this publication may be reproduced, stored in a retrieval system, distributed or transmitted in any form or by any means, including photocopying, recording or other electronic or mechanical methods, without the prior permission of the author, except in the case of brief quotations embodied in critical reviews and certain other non-commercial uses permitted by law.

Disclaimer: This is a work of fiction. Names, characters, businesses, places, events and incidents are either the products of the author's imagination or used in a fictitious manner. Any resemblance to actual persons, living or dead, or actual events is purely coincidental.

Dedicated to Mousey

SD Tanner

Table of Contents

AUTHOR'S NOTE	1
PROLOGUE	3
CHAPTER ONE: Wednesday's Child (Leon)	5
CHAPTER TWO: Blinded by the sight (Twenty-one)	8
CHAPTER THREE: Siren's song (Steve)	17
CHAPTER FOUR: Friendly fire (Jonesy)	25
CHAPTER FIVE: Twilight Flight (John)	32
CHAPTER SIX: Gift wrapped (Leon)	38
CHAPTER SEVEN: Homeward bound (Steve)	48
CHAPTER EIGHT: Step up or out (Jonesy)	55
CHAPTER NINE: Graduation Day (Dayton)	62
CHAPTER TEN: Home Sweet Home (Leon)	71
CHAPTER ELEVEN: Until death do us part (Jonesy)	79
CHAPTER TWELVE: A little respect (Jo)	90
CHAPTER THIRTEEN: Hard landing (Leon)	99
CHAPTER FOURTEEN: Waking nightmare (Ally)	108
CHAPTER FIFTEEN: Born again (Steve)	117
CHAPTER SIXTEEN: Eyes without a face (Ark)	122
CHAPTER SEVENTEEN: Lost in the city (Bill)	131
CHAPTER EIGHTEEN: Witch under the bed (Dayton)	145
CHAPTER NINETEEN: Last man standing (Leon)	152
CHAPTER TWENTY: Sight to behold (Lexie)	159
CHAPTER TWENTY-ONE: Stepping up (Jonesy)	168
CHAPTER TWENTY-TWO: Bolt hole in hell (Leon)	175
CHAPTER TWENTY-THREE: Lemmings (Lexie)	185
CHAPTER TWENTY-FOUR: No place to run (Leon)	197
CHAPTER TWENTY-FIVE: Moving on (Bill)	205
CHAPTER TWENTY-SIX: Bloodless coup (Ark)	212
CHAPTER TWENTY-SEVEN: Earth redefined (Leon)	220
CHAPTER TWENTY-EIGHT: Mankind redefined (Jonesy)	229
CHAPTER TWENTY-NINE: Running blind (Bill)	239
CHAPTER THIRTY: New Army (Leon)	251
EPILOGUE (Steve)	259

AUTHOR'S NOTE

To keep the action exciting this story is told through multiple points of view. Please see the character name in the Chapter heading to know which person is narrating.

For other series by SD Tanner, please check out the Hunter Wars series.

I really hope you enjoy the Navigator series.

SD Tanner

PROLOGUE

The blue planet was covered in water and wide expanses of rich earth. Lifeforms were already living on the land and in the sea, but it would be millennia before it would erupt with even more life, and a single species would dominate. Civilizations would grow and die before it would be time, but when it was, they would harvest the planet and take everything it had to offer. All it took was a little forward planning.

SD Tanner

CHAPTER ONE:
Wednesday's Child
(Leon)

It was Wednesday. Wednesday's child was full of woe, but that only worked for the day you were born, and not the day you died.

His knees were pressing into the hard, rocky ground and his face was covered. With his head bent, his hands were tied behind his back, and men were talking in a language he didn't understand. He assumed Billy and Tuck were next to him, and they would also be on their knees with their hands bound together. Brief gusts of wind were causing the sand on the surface of the land to skitter, and he could hear an animal screaming in fear somewhere in the compound. At least he hoped it was an animal.

They shouldn't have been caught so easily. Mike had been driving the HUMVEE, and they were heading to the forward operating base. The area was supposed to be relatively secure, and the RPG had caught them by surprise. It had hit the front of the truck, flipping it over, and it had landed on its side with a sickening crunch. The enemy had literally swarmed them in numbers he'd never dealt with before, and there'd been no time to react before they were roughly dragged out of the badly damaged vehicle. Under the crush of arms, legs and demanding hands, they'd been stripped of their weapons and thrown into a truck, trussed like the prisoners they now were.

Mike hadn't been in the truck with him, only Billy and Tuck, and he couldn't work out whether he was dead or in another vehicle. With what felt like a scarf tied around his face, he hadn't been able to see anything, and trapped in the back of the truck, they'd whispered urgently to one another about what would happen next. Their best-case scenario was they would find a way to escape, but more likely they would be held prisoner, potentially for years. Their families would plead and the government would negotiate, but before that happened, he expected to be tortured for information he didn't have. It was every soldier's nightmare to be caught by the enemy, held against their will, and unable to defend themselves.

The truck had rumbled along slowly, and every unpredictable bump had jarred him. His body felt bruised, but adrenalin was overriding any injuries he might have. When the truck had finally stopped, he'd been hauled outside and dumped to the ground. Someone had pulled him onto his knees, and while he was forced to kneel with his head bent, their captors seemed to be arguing about something

His mind drifted to Amelia and their unborn son. The only reason he knew they were having a boy was the excited call they'd managed to have three weeks earlier. She'd fallen pregnant in the first week they'd known one another, and they'd married only two weeks before he left for his tour. Life was tough and there was never enough money. All they had was a small one-bedroom apartment in Seattle, and now he needed to scrape together enough cash to find them a house. Amelia and his son needed him, and he frantically tried to think of a way to escape.

The scarf was suddenly yanked from his head, and blinking to clear his vision, he looked around. They'd been taken to a compound of low, flat roofed, shanty houses, and there were at least forty enemy soldiers surrounding them. They were all heavily armed with a wide range of old guns, some of which he didn't even recognize.

The skinny men all looked the same, and they were no more than ten feet away, staring at them with expressions he couldn't read. Without warning, his head was yanked abruptly to the left, and he felt something scrape against the extended tendons on his neck. Desperately moving his eyes, he saw a flat blade reaching from his shoulder. Two weights clamped hard on his calves, and he was held firmly in position. The blade began to move back and forth, crudely tearing into his flesh, and a warm wetness spread down his chest.

"No!" He roared angrily.

Fighting against the steel grip holding him in place, he heard Billy begin to pray.

CHAPTER TWO:
Blinded by the sight
(Twenty-one)

"Nav Two One, do you copy?" The smooth voice asked.

When she didn't answer, it said more urgently, "Nav Two One, I repeat, do you copy?"

Running hard, she wished Ark would shut up. She was in full combat gear and that was never comfortable. The first layer was a body stocking filled with microscopic wires that measured every detail of her physical condition, and allowed her to control the screens no one else could see. The next layer was made up of hydraulic based rods designed to give her a strength and speed she wouldn't otherwise naturally have. The final layer of her gear was a liquid-based armor, reinforced by additional plates strapped across her chest, shoulders and thighs. Whenever she was hit by a bullet or a sharp blow, that area on her armor would stiffen with the impact. Strapped on top of all of the layers was a small oxygen tank to supplement her breathing when needed, and she had a wide flat water pack on her back. Several heavy weapons were attached to her arms, and she carried additional ammo around her waist. All up her kit weighed over two hundred pounds, and given she was only a hundred twenty pounds, it would have been impossible to carry it without the added strength of the hydraulics.

"Two One, quit being a pain in the ass," Ark said amiably. "I can see your readings. I know you're conscious and you can hear me."

Ark was her shadow Navigator and he was safe and sound in Johnsondale. Through a collection of three-dimensional screens, he could see what she could. Right now, he would be sitting in his enormous, well-padded chair, observing her visuals, and tracking her ammo and physical condition. It was his job to make sure she didn't miss anything through her visor and to direct her in combat. The visor tech was the whole purpose of the kit she wore, and it gave her advanced vision. She could see through barriers and identify weapons up to three miles away, and if a Navigator was travelling with a military squad, it would be impossible to ambush them in any way. Having little combat experience, Ark helped her to interpret what she was seeing. He'd been a soldier for ten years, until he was wounded in combat and lost both his legs and half of his face. She assumed his face wasn't a pretty sight, but she didn't really know.

Inside her helmet, she could see a collection of screens, but unlike a television, they provided her with a cartoon version of real life, not that she knew what anything really looked like. The pinkish blobs were people, vehicles were outlined bumps, and weapons were highlighted by red circles. The ground was shown as a grid, with outlined lumps and bumps telling her there was a rock or some other impenetrable object in her way. Walls were a greyed area, and she could see the outlines of anything behind them, whether it was a person, furniture or weapons. She could adjust the distance of her visibility, or zoom in on a specific area with a flick of her wrist. Nothing was hidden from her, and even if their enemy buried a bomb, it emitted a signal her visor could interpret.

For all the capabilities a Navigator had, they lacked one critical sense. For the visor to work, her eyes had been modified. Gone were her original dark brown eyes and they'd been replaced with steel-colored orbs. The orbs contained tiny onboard computers that interacted with her visor screens and translated the data into her brain. Without her visor, she was blind and being so new, the technology had other weaknesses. If she kept the visor on for longer than twelve hours, she developed a migraine that was so bad it often left her physically ill.

Still running at twenty miles per hour, she took a drag on her oxygen pipe, and said breathlessly, "I'm busy."

She was busy. Being a civilian and a contractor for CaliTech, she didn't work for the Army. Her job was to test the new technology, not to use it in anger, but the program was failing and the Army were refusing to continue funding. In a desperate attempt to prove it could work, she'd been told to run her tests in combat. The senior executives had assured her she'd be assigned to an army squad, and not expected to undertake missions alone. Their promises had translated to her being dumped at a base, and immediately sent on a mission to retrieve the squad she'd been assigned to, but never met. The technology was so new it hadn't even been announced in the press, and if their combat testing failed, it might never be.

This wasn't what she'd signed up for, and part of her was angry at being forced into active duty. She wasn't even a soldier. Being born blind had meant she'd lived a sheltered life with her overprotective parents. Determined to strike out on her own, two years earlier she'd moved in with her sister, Shelley. She and Shelley were close, and it had been working out well until her sister had died in a car accident. Her parents had told her to move in with them again, but she hadn't wanted to. For a while she'd lived on her savings, but when she began to run out of money, she'd looked for a job and found CaliTech. The only qualification she'd needed to get the job was to be willing to have her eyes replaced with the computerized orbs.

"You've got forty-five people half a mile ahead. All are armed with AK-47s, and our three guys are in the middle of it," Ark said steadily.

She felt a flutter of anxiety. "What do I do?"

"Two of them are also armed with fifty cals and one has an RPG," Ark replied. "You need to target them first."

No amount of armor would protect her from .50-cal weapons or an RPG, and she stopped and stood with her legs astride, adjusting the distance on her visor. The scene in front of her was immediately overlaid with a grid, and she could see the weapons and position of every person standing around the three men on their knees. Their weapons glowed eerily on her screen, and if she tapped the person, a popup appeared with a description of their weapon, ammo, recent use, distance to her and threat level.

Tapping her screen, she targeted the two men with the .50-cal guns and the one with the RPG. If anyone was watching her, they'd think she was pointing at nothing, but the sensor wires in her gear relayed the message to the onboard computer in her orbs and visor. The computer detected a metal blade was being held against the neck of one of the men, and she could guess what was happening. They were executing the man in the crudest way possible, and a flash of indignant anger cut through her anxiety.

Raising her right arm, she deliberately kept her voice calm. "Auto target."

The main gun was fitted to her right forearm. It fired rapid or single shots, and the bullet would travel down her arm, exiting through a barrel built into her heavily protected gloves. Auto targeting wasn't ideal, but it was all she really knew how to do with any certainty. She wasn't a soldier, and nor was she trained to act like one. She often wondered what she'd gotten herself into when she agreed to become a tester for their technology. Given she was already blind, agreeing to replace her eyes with steel orbs had been a no-brainer, but now she realized CaliTech would own her forever. The technology didn't maintain itself, and she needed their ongoing medical and technical support. If she ever wanted to be free of CaliTech, then she'd have to be willing to be blind again. They would remove her orbs, take away her visor, and give her useless prosthetic eyeballs.

"Take the shots," Ark ordered. "And then move at top speed to the compound."

"You mean shoot the assholes and then run at the bad guys, right?" She asked dourly.

Without waiting to hear Ark's reply, she squeezed her fist, using her index finger to press a trigger on her glove at the base of her hand. With the one movement, she'd instructed her weapon to fire at the designated targets. Even through the heavy armor, she could feel the buck of the gun and the bullets leaving the chamber. The hydraulics automatically moved her arm, and through her visor, she watched all three targets fall as quickly as three shots could leave her weapon.

When she hesitated to move, Ark shouted through her earpiece, "Go! Go! Go!"

The urgency in his voice raised her anxiety levels another notch, and without any thought, she began to sprint towards the enemy.

"Fire! Fire!" Ark roared.

The screen on her visor filled with bright, sparking lights, and she knew she was being fired at. As she ran at twenty-five miles an hour into the flashing, she felt her body being thrown by each bullet that found its mark. Her armor was hardening all over her body, but she ran on relentlessly. The armor might stop the bullets from penetrating, but the sharp impact made it bulge into her body, which could leave her bruised or potentially injured.

"Can't see!" She screamed.

There was so much gunfire her visor was becoming nothing more than brilliant white light. She was panting and her rising panic threatened to engulf her. All she wanted to do was fall to the ground and curl up into a ball. She didn't want this job. She was contracted to test the equipment and provide feedback to the designers. When they'd told her she was assigned to an active military squad, she'd argued she wasn't a soldier and had no interest in being one. The sleazy guy from Legal had pointed to a clause in her contract about 'Advanced Testing'. The equally sleazy Accounts rep had given her a spiel about her country needing her. They'd made it clear to her that she could either do this, or they would send her back to a world of never ending darkness.

"Calm down, Two One," Ark said steadily. "Auto targeting is on. Your onboard computer is firing at will."

Without her noticing, while she ran, her right arm with the primary weapon was moving under the control of her visor computer. It was returning fire with deadly accuracy, and her screen was becoming less filled with flashing lights. When her screen flashed she was low on ammo, she continued to run and reload at the same time. In just over a minute, she'd cleared the half-mile across the sand and was almost on top of the enemy position. The three men, once trapped in the middle of the group, were now on their feet and were fighting with the enemy. Her visor computer recognized them as belonging to her, and she knew there was no chance she would accidentally shoot them.

Her guys were moving away from the enemy, leaving a trail of injured and dead people behind them. She continued to fire and soon more bullets were directed at the enemy. Her guys were using the enemies' weapons against them. Her screen was flashing. She was low on ammo again, but she'd used everything she had. Her screen began to flash red, and now she was low on power too. Another glitch with the technology was when it was used at full force it drank the power packs. She hated the gear, it was buggy. If she ran out of power, she'd lose the hydraulics and eventually her visor, which would leave her blind and unable to move. Realizing she had no more than a few minutes of power left, she began to panic.

Ark could see her vitals and she heard him speak. "Stay calm, Two One. You're doing fine."

"Easy for you to say."

Now out of ammo, she swung her right arm at an enemy target next to her as she ran past him. Her hydraulics could deliver a clout equivalent to being hit by a moving truck, and the man was thrown from his feet. Forced to resort to hand-to-hand combat, she grabbed another man in front of her, and slammed him into the ground. Without hesitating, she stomped on him heavily, and then continued towards her guys who were still firing and retreating.

As she moved closer to them, she shouted, "Where are they going?"

"There's vehicles behind the houses," Ark replied. "Follow them."

There were at least ten enemies still surrounding her, and she began to swing her arms wildly, catching them with hard and fast blows. Her visor was now emitting a high pitch trill to warn her she was almost out of power.

"Ark, I'm losing it!"

Continuing to punch out wildly at the bodies around her, she felt the power cut off, and dropped to her knees with the weight of the gear.

"Ark, I'm down!"

Her visor went blank and without it, she was blind whether she wore it or not.

"Ark," she whispered breathlessly, knowing she was caught.

"You're okay. Don't panic," Ark replied steadily.

Before she could call him an asshole, she ran out of power and her radio mike went dead.

Confused and frightened, she whispered, "Ark?"

CHAPTER THREE:
Siren's song
(Steve)

The woman on the television was clearly panic-stricken, and her usually immaculate makeup was shiny with sweat. On his wide flat-screen, little clumps of mascara were visible around her eyes, making her look slightly clown-like. Outside his apartment in downtown Albuquerque, the sirens were wailing, one on top of another, until the noise took on an almost insane rhythm he could dance to.

"Police are reporting an escalating number of domestic violence incidents taking place across the city. In downtown Albuquerque there are thousands of attacks being reported, and no one knows why."

It had started with murders being reported less than an hour ago, but now the disheveled looking news reporter was telling them not to call '911'. Apparently, they were busy and he scratched at his head irritably. This morning he'd woken up with a blinding headache, and his wife, Lucy, had told him to stay in bed. Initially he hadn't wanted to. He'd only just been promoted to Claim Processing Manager, and he didn't want to jeopardize his Christmas bonus, but since this morning his headache had evolved into a full-scale migraine. Now his head was so itchy he was contemplating attacking it with a fork.

"Albuquerque isn't the only city to be affected. There are reports from all the major cities of a massive number of domestic attacks. People are murdering their family members in their own homes, and others are attacking strangers in the street. Police are advising everyone to stay in their homes unless they're attacked, but they aren't telling us where anyone can go to be safe. Hospitals are operating at capacity, but even they are not immune to the attacks. There are reports of incidents..."

The over-sized woman on his forty-inch flat screen had stopped talking, and was frantically looking over her shoulder at something happening behind her. Still sitting with his feet propped up in his favorite lay-z-boy armchair, next to his elbow was an abandoned bowl of cold spaghetti. He couldn't remember when he'd heated it up, but he noted there was a fork stuck in the hard, sticky mess. Pulling the fork out, and not bothering to wipe it clean, he rammed it against his tingling scalp, and rubbed the prongs vigorously into his skin. The scraping noise echoed through his head, making him drill the fork in even deeper. It hurt less than he expected, and he continued to dig at the tingling sensation, until it was overridden by the feeling of metal on bone.

"Oh my God, we have to get out of here..."

The high-pitched tone of the woman's voice caught his attention again and he forgot about the fork. Outside he could hear sporadic gunfire and it annoyed him. It was interrupting the pleasant rhythm of the sirens and giving his music a rap feel. He didn't like rap, the jerkiness was jarring and he couldn't dance to it. The woman on the screen had disappeared and the camera was pointing downwards at the road. Bored with the view, he took the remote from his lap and began flicking through the stations, but whenever he found one, the emergency broadcast image would appear. He continued to change the channel, but soon all of them were displaying the same image.

Bored with the television, he cranked the arm on the side of his chair, flicking the footrest down. Lucy should be home soon and he wanted to see her. They'd only been married for two years. They'd met at his father's sixtieth birthday party in Bernalillo, and it had been a whirlwind courtship. She was a diminutive brunette with perfect curves, and it was a second marriage for both of them. He supposed they'd both been lonely, but whatever the reason for their attraction to one another, they'd been married within a year of meeting. Being in their mid-thirties, they were keen to start a family, and his recent promotion meant Lucy could quit work.

Wandering into the bathroom, he studied his face in the large square mirror over the sink. He wasn't a classically handsome man, but with his full head of hair and craggy features, he wasn't unattractive either. It was then he heard something dripping, and glanced down at the white porcelain bowl. It was streaked with red, and turning his head slightly, he noticed blood was dripping past his ear and splashing into the sink. Lucy was a fussy housekeeper and she wouldn't be happy with the mess he was making.

The blood reminded him of something he was supposed to do, and he walked across the small apartment to their bedroom. Sliding aside the mirrored door to their wardrobe, he looked up at the neat rows of boxes above the hanging clothes. Ignoring his initial impulse to carefully search through the tidy shelf, he began to tug at the cardboard and plastic boxes, throwing them to the ground. The box he wanted was tucked away at the back where Lucy would never find it. Finally, he found what he was looking for, and it was an unremarkable looking shoebox he knew Lucy would never look in. Sitting on the bed with the box in his lap, he carelessly flicked the lid off, and inside was a Ruger P95 with fifty rounds of ammunition.

Lifting the gun from the box, he used the barrel to scratch his scalp again, then checked to see if it was loaded and it was. Putting the gun on the bed, he fumbled at the bottom of the wardrobe for his most hardwearing walking boots and tugged them on. While he laced them, the blood from his scalp ran down his face, dripped from the end of his nose, and landed on the top of his steel-capped boots. Ignoring the blood, he decided to put on his coat. It wasn't cold enough to need one, but the pockets were large and deep, and he loaded the gun and extra ammunition inside them.

He was ready to leave and then wondered where he was going. Confused, he sat down on the bed again and listened to the sound of gunfire outside. It seemed to be growing and he wondered why. The distinctive sound of a key in their front door lock caught his attention and he heard Lucy's voice.

"Steve! Steve!"

It took a moment for him to realize that was his name, and he looked towards the door. Within a few seconds, Lucy's tiny frame filled the doorway, and she ran forward into his arms.

"Have you seen the news?" She asked in a breathless voice. "I ran all the way home. I tried to call, but the phones aren't working." Beginning to sob, she clutched at his neck, burying her face in his heavy coat. "People are killing one another everywhere. I was sitting at my desk and people started showing one another news reports on their phones. I didn't wait. I was so worried about you…I…I ran."

His hand was still in his pocket, wrapped around his Ruger, and he didn't know why. He loved Lucy. They were going get a house with a mortgage in the suburbs, have a couple of kids, and she was going to become a soccer mom. That was the plan and they were excited about it. He knew the life he'd planned to have, but he didn't recognize this woman anymore.

Lucy pulled back from his coat and stared up at his face worriedly. "Are you okay? Why are you bleeding? What happened?"

He looked back at her, but her face wasn't familiar. She could have been anyone, in fact she reminded him of the woman on the television. Her dark hair was pulled back into an untidy ponytail, and long wisps were trailing down her cheeks. Black smudges of mascara dotted her cheekbones, giving her a raccoon face, and the idea she was a small, furry animal made him chuckle softly to himself.

"What are you laughing at?" She asked warily.

She slowly stood up from the bed and carefully stepped back towards the bedroom door.

"Steve?"

Her eyes were wide with fear, and he could see tension was building in her curvaceous body. He remembered having sex with her, only now their moments of intimacy struck him as absurd. The whole sexual act was ridiculous, and he wondered why he'd ever thought it was important. Thinking about the jiggling motion made him laugh out loud.

"Oh no," she whispered. "Steve…"

His scalp was itching again, and still holding the gun, he pulled his hand from his pocket and used it to scratch the spot vigorously.

"Put the gun down, Steve."

Her tone irritated him. He wasn't doing anything wrong, his head was itchy was all. She was always nagging him about something. According to her, he made a mess of the bathroom, left dishes in the sink, and didn't listen to her when she told him what was good for him. Lucy annoyed him, but he was only just realizing it and he glared at her resentfully.

She must have sensed the change in his mood and she cried, "No, Steve, don't." Giving him a pleading look, she said desperately, "I'll leave and I won't come back. I promise. Just let me go. Please."

He could let her leave and then she wouldn't be so irritating. Pursing his lips while he studied her, another itch began to tingle down his spine, and it was even more annoying than the one on his scalp.

"Why are you bleeding? What's happened to you?"

Her comment seemed at odds with her previous one, and he looked at her quizzically. His life seemed to be shrinking into a series of competing needs. His back was itchier than his scalp, and he wondered how he could scratch it. Seeing the gun in his hand, he rubbed it vigorously against the back of his thick coat. It helped a little, but it didn't make the annoying sensation go away.

Lucy must have seen his action as her opportunity to escape and she turned and ran. Her sudden movement crystalized something in his addled mind, and he leapt from the bed after her. Their apartment only had a small combined kitchen and lounge area leading to the front door. Heading for the door, Lucy tripped over a low footstool and fell in a sprawling heap.

Seeing her lying on the ground, with her body half twisted to face him, he felt a deep surge of distaste. It wasn't hatred or even anger, only that he didn't want her around anymore. She didn't belong here and she should leave. A small voice inside him suggested he should let her go, but he didn't think that was good enough. She shouldn't be here, and by here, he didn't mean in their apartment. She simply shouldn't exist. Somehow her presence threatened his, and if he had to choose, then she would be the one to go.

Lifting his hand with the gun, he aimed it directly at her.

She raised a hand to her face, as if she could protect herself against a bullet. "No, no, Steve, don't. I'm sorry."

Her apology momentarily confused him, and then he decided she was apologizing for being somewhere she didn't belong. It was good she understood she didn't have the right to exist, and he pulled the trigger. He'd never fired the gun much, and yet the noise and buck of the weapon felt familiar in a way it shouldn't have. The bullet ripped through the air, sliced into her hand, and then penetrated her face.

He leaned over her collapsed body, only vaguely interested in the effect of the bullet, and could hear her breathing in ragged gasps. The bullet had torn through her forehead, leaving a bloodied trail from her eyebrow to her hairline. She wasn't dead, in fact he doubted the wound would kill her. He contemplated shooting her again, but the sound of gunfire outside the apartment caught his attention. There was something he was supposed to do, and it was related to the sirens and bullets.

Stepping over Lucy's bleeding body, he opened the door to their apartment, and walked into the corridor outside.

CHAPTER FOUR:
Friendly fire
(Jonesy)

The precinct was going crazy. People were running from phones to their computer screens and back again. It had started an hour ago, and the noise level was now so high he couldn't hear himself think. The dispatch center had lit up like a Christmas tree with panicked calls from people across Albuquerque. Even now, the large television screen in the main office area in the precinct was constantly playing news reports. It was as if a switch had been flicked, and the entire city had erupted into domestic violence. People were calling in, sounding desperate and saying someone was trying to kill them. During some of the calls, the person was heard being murdered, while still pleading for help from the operator. Cars that had been sent to addresses were disappearing on route, and no one could raise them on the radio. Since the calls had started, over half of the cops on the beat were now missing.

At fifty-five years of age, he was far too old to be out on the beat, and had long settled into a desk job processing paperwork. They used a lot less paper now and it was mostly electronic forms, but the intent was the same. Every action they took in the department had to be recorded, justified, explained and approved. It was a boring job, but he was happy with his nine to five routine. For the first time in thirty years, he was able to go home every night to his wife, Jenny. It had been a while since he'd needed to carry a gun and he didn't miss it. A cop's life wasn't like some cheesy seventies television show, there weren't bad guys on every corner, and mostly all he'd ever dealt with were idiots. The way he saw it, he'd done his fair share of picking up the drunks and hustling gangs of youths from dark corners.

He hadn't really wanted to get involved in some huge scene, and had assumed it was just one of those days. A full moon really did bring out the lunatics, but it was broad daylight and there was no moon. Tucked away in the corner of the office where no one ever looked, he watched the increasing panic in front of him. He'd long lost the need to appear tough, and he'd been trying to ignore the chaos building around him. These days he was too tired to beat his chest at all the other chimps in the pack, but when even the rookie cops began gearing up, it was their tense faces that finally tore his well-padded ass from his chair.

Removing his reading glasses, he put them away in their case so they wouldn't get scratched. Jenny was an excellent cook, her homemade pasta was to die for, and given his cholesterol results he very well might. He'd put on at least fifty pounds since he'd last been on the streets, and his doctor had put him on statins for the rest of his life, effectively giving him permission to indulge knowing there would be no consequences. Tugging his jacket from the slightly fuzzy fabric covering his padded swivel chair, he sighed and prepared to step into the fray. He really was too old to join in, but he'd been a cop for thirty years, and he wasn't going to abandon his city if it really needed him.

Walking across to the Commander, he waited until she'd finished issuing orders to her deputies. When she finally turned to look at him, he smiled wanly. "I'm trained and I can use a gun. What can I do?"

He expected her to tell him he was too old, too fat and too out-of-date, but she didn't. "Find yourself a rookie and keep them alive," she replied tersely.

"Do you know what's going on?"

Her pale face seemed to become even more waxen, and he realized she was frightened. "No, I don't. Half the cops out there are missing, and even the ones we find keep disappearing again."

Her name was Jo, short for Josephine, and she was usually sharp, blunt and never flustered, but now she placed the palm of hand against her chest, and seemed to fold slightly into herself. "I don't understand. I'm losing my officers. The operators have heard gunfire in the squad cars." Shaking her head, she muttered, "They've heard them killing one another."

"What have you heard from the other precincts?"

"Not much. No one's had time to talk other than to report the same problems."

These days the news and other social media provided the most up-to-date information, and he swung his heavy, six foot three inch frame to face the flat screen television mounted on the wall in the main room. A nervous blonde newsreader was looking over her shoulder anxiously, then the camera must have been dropped, and all he could see was a shot of the asphalt road.

Turning away from the screen, he asked, "And what exactly is the problem?"

"I don't know. An hour ago, the switchboards jammed with calls about attacks happening on the street and in people's homes. Family members, neighbors and strangers just started attacking one another. We have reports of people being killed with guns, knives, and other weapons. Men, women and children are being slaughtered. We contacted University Hospital to ask them what condition the survivors were in, but we never got a sensible reply. All they told us was they had people with near fatal injuries, and then they came under attack as well...by their own staff, patients and visitors."

"What does HQ say about it?"

Jo gave him a look of disbelief. "We lost contact with them about twenty minutes ago, but before we did they had nothing useful to say. It seems every station across the country is in the same position, and they had no useful advice to offer other than to deal with it."

"What do you mean you lost contact with them?"

"They're not answering our calls anymore and the radio is down."

It was his turn to give her a look of complete disbelief. "What are you saying? We're on our own? Where's the National Guard? We don't have the resources to deal with this level of crisis. This isn't what we're designed to do."

"You're preaching to the choir," she replied worriedly. Leaning closer to him, she added quietly, "But what if this is a terrorist attack? What if the bad guys put something in the water that's making people crazy? What if this is the result of a smart bomb of some sort?"

He knew she'd just voiced her greatest fear that their country was under attack in a way they couldn't defend against. Their own people were killing one another with no concern about the consequences. It made no sense and he couldn't rule out a terrorist attack either. "It's plausible, but I'm not sure it matters."

"What do you mean?"

Glancing back at the television screen, he noticed it was now only displaying the emergency broadcast image. "It doesn't matter why people are killing one another. All we need to know is they are, and they're doing it in numbers we can't respond to. We haven't got enough cops to deal with this."

She nodded. "It's not just that. I don't think the ones we have are immune either. We've heard them attacking one another on the radio. No one can be trusted."

"What's the emergency procedure?"

"For this?" She asked in surprise. "There isn't one. You're talking about large numbers of people randomly killing one another for no reason. All of our procedures assume there's a level of government left standing that can implement a state of emergency, but if the attackers are randomly across the entire population, then the whole system falls apart. When I was able to contact the Chief, he was trying to contact the State Police and National Guard. The Emergency Operations Center should be up and running, but I haven't heard whether we've managed to get through to them yet. If I don't hear from them, then it means we don't have State Police, an Army or a National Guard."

Their protocols in a state of emergency assumed at least one of the many levels of government and protective forces would be intact. It was a reasonable assumption, but it didn't work if they couldn't trust their own people. For the first time since the attacks started, he began to worry about his wife. He needed to talk to her and he pulled his phone from his pocket.

Jo watched him and said bluntly, "That won't work. The network is jammed."

Tapping the screen to call his wife, he held the phone to his ear. All he heard was the irritating sharp beep of an engaged tone. "I need to go home and check she's okay. She should be in our apartment in Sawmill in the city."

Jo nodded curtly. "Okay, but take a rookie with you."

"What do you expect me to do out there?"

The queue of people needing to talk to Jo had been growing from the moment he'd started their conversation. Clearly becoming distracted, she replied, "I don't know. Just...just try to serve and protect...and stay in radio contact. I'll let you know as soon as I get some answers from somewhere."

Continuing to dial Jenny on his mobile phone, he left the precinct office area and headed to the locker room, looking for a gun and a vest. Every locker was open, and bits of kit were all over the floor, where there were a dozen people picking at the discarded items. Deciding he could live without a vest, he walked across the hall to the armory. The window was open, but no one was there and it was immediately obvious why. The usually packed shelves were empty and he guessed they had nothing left. With so many cops out on the streets, and no weapons left at the precinct, they were vulnerable to attack. Fortunately, he kept his own private arsenal in his Chevrolet Malibu.

Walking back to the locker room, he boomed, "I have my own personal vehicle and weapons. I need a rookie with me."

All faces turned to stare, and a young woman strode towards him. "I'm still in basic training."

"Can you handle a gun?"

"Yeah, my Dad taught me how to do that."

He looked the dark haired girl up and down, and decided she looked fit and strong. "Okay, then let's go."

Following him down the corridor towards the parking lot, she easily kept pace while he felt slightly winded. "Where are we going?"

Other than finding Jenny, he wasn't sure what he could do on the streets. Jo had told him to serve and protect, but he didn't know what that would entail. "I don't know until we get out there and see what's really going on."

When they reached his Malibu, she said, "I'm Jasmine, but everyone calls me Jas."

Opening the trunk to his car, he lifted the base, revealing a Glock in its holster, an AR-15 and a Remington 870 shotgun hidden inside. Strapping the Glock to his hip, he handed Jas the AR-15 and ammo. "I'm Harry Jones, but everyone calls me Jonesy."

CHAPTER FIVE:
Twilight Flight
(John)

He hated being forced to arrive at the airport two hours in advance, then having his possessions shoved down a dark hole, being frisked or x-rayed, and left to wait on an uncomfortable chair, eating over-priced food and drinking coffee from a cardboard cup. Unfortunately flying across the country came with his job as a retail specialist. As the Operations Quality Assessor, he travelled to all their outlets to check planograms, stock, staff performance and customer satisfaction levels. The excessive travel demands meant his wife and three kids got to live in suburban luxury in Philadelphia, while he moved from one hotel to the next.

Where he'd gained nearly a hundred pounds eating hotel food, his wife, Lily, was still a dark haired beauty. When they'd married, he'd looked like a well-built, blond-haired linebacker, but those days were long gone. Back then he could pull any woman he wanted, but now he spilled over his narrow seat, and the redheaded woman next to him was actively trying not to touch any part of him. He didn't blame her, his shirt was pitted with stains from his lunch, and even with the cool air pumping from the overhead vent, he was sweating profusely. Thinking of Lily made his mouth pull into a grimace. He was pretty sure she was seeing someone else. On his most recent trip home, he'd noticed a collection of new lingerie drying in their shared bathroom. It was lacy and red with matching stockings, and it certainly hadn't been worn for his benefit.

Part of him wondered if he should lose some weight to try and rekindle their marriage. A larger part of him thought she should be grateful for the lifestyle he worked so hard to provide. Resentment bubbled up deep inside his chest, and he stared out of the window miserably. Being a regular flyer, he always requested to sit over the wing of the plane to give himself slightly more room. He found getting in and out of his chair embarrassing, so he always booked a window seat. The chair was too small for him to move his body in any way, and he turned his head further to stare across the wing of the plane. Recoiling in surprise, he banged his shoulder into the redheaded woman next to him. She gave a small indignant squeal, and then began to mop furiously at her dress.

"Be careful," she said sharply.

He turned to look at her heavily made up face, and realized his abrupt movement had made her spill her coffee down the front of her green dress. It was a very low cut number, and the contours of her rounded white breasts disappeared under the clingy fabric. He thought he saw a flash of red lace and it reminded him of Lily.

"Err, sorry, I thought I saw something outside."

"Well, you're looking at something right now, you pervert."

"No, no, I was just looking at what you were doing."

"And copping a look," she replied archly.

The flash of red lace had only brought Lily to his mind, but he couldn't tell the woman that had made his stomach turn. Lily embodied everything that was failing in his life. He was fat, unattractive to women, his wife was screwing around, and all of it was making him feel utterly inadequate. The redheaded woman next to him might not find him attractive, but he didn't want her either.

Sighing, he returned to looking out of the window. The flat steel wing reached into the distance, and there was nothing other than puffy, white clouds beyond it. He couldn't see the ground below and he found the view boring. Whatever he thought he'd seen was either gone, or it was never there in the first place. He thought he might as well check out the inflight entertainment, and as he fumbled with his headsets, a movement outside the window caught his attention again. This time he definitely saw something. It was black and it moved across his window with lightning speed.

"What the hell was that?"

"What was what?" The woman replied tersely.

"I saw something go past my window."

The woman sighed irritably. "I don't know. I can't see past you."

Her reference to his size didn't go unnoticed, and he tried to sink lower into his chair, but his knees banged awkwardly into the seat in front of him. She was being decidedly rude and he didn't want to talk to her. Ignoring her jibe, he stared out of the window, and something black flashed past, only this time it skittered across the long wing. When it turned and stood in the middle of the wing, he noticed its claws had dug deep into the metal. It had skinny arms and legs with knobby joints, its head was round and featureless, and the torso was a solid curved oval. The face was smooth with molded looking eyes, nose and mouth, but it didn't appear to have any ears. Lifting its scrawny arms wide, a webbed sheet appeared under each. The creature dropped to its knees, crawling along the wing until it tilted its head into the engine, and then it was gone.

Swiveling his head sharply, he looked around to see if anyone else had noticed the creature. In the seat next to the redheaded woman, a man was docilely eating from an airline snack pack. The droning of the engines eliminated most sound, but he could still hear the people talking behind him. Worried the creature may have damaged the engine, he knew he had to get out of his seat and speak to an attendant.

Unbuckling his extended seatbelt, he said, "I have to get up."

The woman sighed irritably and unbuckled her own seatbelt. Nudging the man eating from the box, she muttered, "He needs to get out."

Both of them moved the items from their fold down trays and shuffled out of their seats. Getting out of an airline chair was always difficult for him, and he flipped the side arms upward to give himself more room. Using the chairs in front to lever his body along the row, they bent backwards heavily, and the people in them looked up at him in surprise. He was making a spectacle of himself and he knew it. Flushed with the effort and the embarrassment, he finally stood sideways in the narrow corridor. He shuffled along it trying not to nudge the people on either side, until he found himself standing in the relatively open area next to the exits.

The cabin crew were still wheeling their trolleys at the back of the plane, offering their lackluster meals to bored passengers. The people sitting next to the exit had wrapped blankets around their legs, making it hard for him to know where their feet were. Leaning down, he peered out of the window on the door, hoping to catch a glimpse of the odd creature. The wing of the plane was empty again, and he wondered if he'd seen anything at all.

Now he was up he decided he might as well go to the bathroom. He didn't need to, but at least it justified moving everyone in his aisle. If he was honest, he didn't really want to face the disapproving look he would get from the redheaded woman. Lily glared at him enough as it was. Her tiny sighs and disappointed face was enough to tell him she thought he was failing her. It didn't seem fair to him. She lived in a beautiful four-bedroom home, the kids went to private schools, and she even had her own sports car. He'd achieved more than he ever thought possible for a high school jock, and he wished she'd cut him some slack.

He was standing at the front of the aisle looking at the rows of faces in front of him. Some were staring back at him with what he thought were disgusted expressions, others were reading or watching the screen in front of them. It was daylight, and the cabin was flooded with light from the windows, when suddenly everything went black.

"What the hell?"

The plane dipped in a sharp descent and he fell forwards, landing heavily against the people seated next to the exit. The armrest was digging into his side and people were beginning to howl in fear. The plane's sharp descent didn't stop, and despite his bulk, he felt himself beginning to float from the row of chairs. He was airborne in moments, and his body began to roll, slamming him against the overhead lockers, windows and chairs. As if he was crowd surfing at a concert, he rolled along the top of the long line of passenger seats, hitting people with his flailing arms and legs.

The screaming intensified. He was tearing through oxygen masks that had dropped from the ceiling of the plane, and his head was being hammered into overhead lockers and windows. His last sight through the window was that of the creature, only it wasn't alone. Clinging to the wing of the plane were hundreds of black bodies.

CHAPTER SIX:
Gift wrapped
(Leon)

With his heart beating rapidly in his chest, blood was running freely down his neck and drenching his shirt. He suspected it hurt, but his brain and body were still so fueled with adrenalin he couldn't feel a thing. Billy was driving the old Toyota pickup, and Tuck was crouched down in the back of the truck with him, firing steadily at the enemy. Of the forty or so men that had surrounded them, thanks to their combined efforts, less than a dozen were left standing. As Billy drove around the shanty houses, there was a black clad body wearing fitted headgear lying prone in the sand.

Navigators, he thought irritably, what next? From the little he'd been told, there were currently only a small number of fully trained Navigators in existence. He'd never even heard of the technology until he was called into a briefing by his Company Commander, and was told one had been assigned to his squad. His Commanding Officer had said they were a top secret capability, still being piloted under tight security, but if they tested the tech in combat theater, then it wouldn't be long before everyone knew about it.

Billy stopped the truck next to the black clad body, Tuck kept shooting, while he leaned down over the tailgate and tried to haul the Navigator into the back of the truck. The body was heavier than he expected, and he braced his legs against the edge of the vehicle. Seeing him struggling, Tuck briefly ceased firing to help him pull the body on board. The Navigator wasn't being any help, and he wondered if the guy was injured. Shuffling on his ass to the driver's back window, he banged on the glass and indicated they needed to get the hell out of dodge. Billy obliged, and the truck accelerated away from the compound.

"What a fuck up," Tuck complained.

The truck was bumping furiously along the dirt track, leaving a trail of billowing fine sand behind it. Putting his hand on his neck, he felt a soft wetness, and decided they hadn't cut deep enough to cause any real damage. He had to admit, seeing the Navigator sprinting to their position with all guns blazing was both a relief and an impressive sight. Wearing fitted black armor, with a full facemask molded to the contours of his skull, the guy looked like an angry ninja. Two thick guns were built into each forearm, which puzzled him. Surely the guy could only fire with any accuracy using his dominant hand. He didn't have time to study the Navigator closely, but the facemask didn't seem to have any air holes, and he assumed the gear was supplying him with oxygen.

Continuing to watch for any pursuing enemy, he quickly glanced down at the Navigator still lying on his back, and decided he owed the man a beer.

"What now?" Tuck asked loudly.

"We head back to the base," he replied.

"Do ya reckon they know what's happened?" Tuck asked.

Giving Tuck a confused look, he replied, "They must have seen it happen or they wouldn't have sent the nav." Pointing at the blue sky above them, he added, "They've got satellite eyes in the sky. They know exactly what's happened."

Looking above him, Tuck said vaguely, "Oh, yeah, I guess so." Pointing at the Navigator, he asked, "What about this guy? Do you think he's hurt?"

In the briefing about Navigator technology, he'd been told they were blind. Their natural born eyes had been replaced with silver orbs that interacted with their visor, but if they lost power as this guy had, then they wouldn't be able to see. It was a stupid design. What soldier in their right mind would agree to potentially becoming blind in combat? They were also told not to remove the armor from an injured Navigator. Their armor did stop bullets from any weapon under .50-cal penetrating them, but it didn't stop the possible damage from the impact caused by a lower caliber. The bullet could hit them in a vulnerable area, so that even when the armor hardened, it could bulge deeply into the soft tissue of the Navigator. They were told the impact could cause such massive internal injuries that their armor might be the only thing holding them together. It was another stupid aspect about the design. They couldn't help a Navigator if they were injured in combat. Staring down at the immobilized black body, he realized with over two hundred pounds of gear and no power, the guy was like a turtle stuck on its back.

Shaking his head in disgust, he replied, "It doesn't matter if he is, we can't do anything for him other than to get him outta here."

Looking equally as offended, Tuck asked, "Why the fuck did they design this shit? It's a surefire way to get yourself killed."

"They've got too much money and not enough brains."

He gave up looking at the prone Navigator and stared up at the sky hoping to spot a drone. The Navigator had a small chip inserted into the back of his neck, and the satellites would pick up its low frequency signal. By now, Central Command would know they'd cleared the enemy territory and were on the move.

Seeing a drone heading towards them, he elbowed Tuck. "There you go."

Tuck followed his eyes and nodded. "It was close."

Snorting, he replied dourly, "Not close enough to stop some asshole from nearly cutting off my head with a rusty knife."

"I thought we were goners, and what the hell was Billy praying for?"

He didn't know Billy and he barely knew Tuck. At least he and Tuck had worked in 2nd Platoon for the past three years. Billy had only just finished basic training, and he wasn't too pleased about having a greenhorn assigned to him. Mike wasn't even from his platoon and he hadn't known him at all. He still wasn't sure what had happened to him, but he suspected they'd find his body with their destroyed truck.

He'd been in the army for eight years and this was his fourth combat tour, which made him an experienced veteran. Signing up at the age of twenty-six, he was considered to be an older recruit, but he'd had enough of selling cars for a living. If he was completely honest, he'd been bored and had wanted a change of pace, which the army had certainly given him. Although he'd enjoyed his time in the military, when he was asked if he wanted to sign up again he'd said no. The deployments had been a much-needed break from his small apartment and predictable lifestyle, but now he was married and expecting a baby, his priorities had changed and it was time to move on.

When they finally cleared their way into the small base, a medic walked over to them. "You guys okay?"

Taking his hand from his still bleeding neck, he said, "I had a run in with an asshole and a rusty knife."

Pulling out a small vial, the med tech sprayed his hands with a sheer coating that would both protect and disinfect them. Touching his neck gently, he said, "Doesn't look too bad, but you need to get that patched up and have a tetanus shot." Looking him closely in the eyes, he asked, "Are you in any pain? I can give you something now."

Shaking his head, he said, "Nah, I'm good, but you need to check this nav out."

Several soldiers approached their stolen vehicle, and they carried the prone Navigator to a nearby medical tent. Dumping the body onto a sturdy bed, it groaned under the sudden weight. Starting with the boots and gloves, the medical personnel began to free the Navigator from their heavy gear. This was his first sighting of a Navigator, and he waved away the medic trying to look at his neck. Once the gloves and boots were removed, they began to unbuckle the weapons, armor belt, used power packs and the water bag. Beneath the gear was a fitted black suit with heavier armor strapped to the chest, arms and legs. It looked like a tight wet suit, and he assumed it contained the hydraulics. After unbuckling the removable parts of the armor, a medic had pulled out a large pair of scissors, obviously intending to cut the suit from the Navigator.

"Don't cut that," a voice called out.

Turning, he watched a masculine looking woman with white, sharply cropped hair march into the medical tent. Walking up to the table where the Navigator was lying, she elbowed the medics away and said curtly, "If you cut it, you break it."

Pulling out a thin, pencil shaped unit, she slipped it inside a sleeve on the Navigator's suit and read the display. Nodding brusquely, she said, "All the vitals look good."

Having confirmed the Navigator was safe inside the gear, the woman began to unclip the neck brace and peeled it away from the torso. Through the small gap between the chin and collarbone, he could see the chest was rising and falling as he breathed.

The headgear was a helmet with a large, hinged lower jaw that blended in so well it was almost invisible, and the eyes were covered with a black, glossy wide strip. Once the woman had deftly unclipped the lower jaw on the helmet, he could see the flesh colored skin of the Navigator inside.

Now able to be heard, the Navigator said irritably, "Get me the hell out of this thing."

The woman didn't reply, but continued to gently remove the helmet and visor from the still prone Navigator. To his surprise, the finely boned and highly structured face of a woman with cropped, blonde hair emerged. Instead of eyes, the woman's sockets were filled with light silver colored orbs, and she was blinking rapidly as if the sudden exposure to light was uncomfortable for her.

She continued to complain. "Get this crap off me. I can't fucking move. Get Ark on the grid. I wanna yell at him."

Snapping her chest armor open, the woman pushed her hand under the Navigator's shoulder, helping to free her arm from the heavy suit. Once the woman had both arms free, she began to peel the armored suit from her lower body.

While she roughly threw the lower part of her armor onto the floor, she complained incessantly. "I hate this job. I wanna talk to Ark."

"Stop bitching," the woman replied sternly. "And tell me if anything hurts."

Snorting derisively, the woman replied irritably, "Everything hurts, Donna. I've been stuck in this gear and thrown around like a penny in a can. Who the hell trained this squad?" Starting to remove her hydraulics layer, the woman muttered angrily, "They don't know what they're doing, and they were throwing me around like a sack of dirt."

The hydraulics layer was designed to the woman's exact size and shape. According to his briefing, it was lined with interlocking rods that formed an exoskeleton, complete with hydraulic joints. Working much like a human joint, it had the added benefit of being virtually unbreakable. It meant the joint could take massive impact without injuring the Navigator's limbs, and it gave them the ability to run, jump and carry weights beyond normal human capacity. It was impressive technology, but he wasn't sure it was being used correctly. Apparently the army thought they could create entire battalions of Navigators, effectively replacing the current boots on the ground. While they'd listened to the online tutorial during the briefing, both he and his CO had shared more than a few skeptical looks. Without even discussing it, they'd both agreed that a blind soldier so utterly dependent on a power source was a dead man walking or in this case a dead woman.

Once the woman was free of her hydraulics gear, she began to peel away the thin bodysuit of sensors covering her. When she was finally free of all of her kit, she was left sitting on the table wearing only a small pair of black panties.

"Lie down. I need to check you for injuries," Donna said sternly.

"No," the woman replied abruptly.

Swinging her legs over the side of the table, she slid from the bed and stood unsteadily. Rolling her eyes, Donna said with a sigh, "Lexie, stop being difficult. You're only feeling cranky because you're still full of adrenalin." Now examining her body for bruises or injuries, she added, "You're also standing practically naked in front of about twenty people."

Snorting again, Lexie replied, "I'm only naked, it's not like I'm having sex."

"Oh, is that where you draw the line for having an audience?" Donna asked bluntly.

Screwing up her face, and waving her hand at the room full of people she couldn't see, Lexie replied, "Given I can see through walls, as soon as I'm wearing my visor again, none of you people are gonna have any secrets from me."

The Navigator who'd disrupted their enemy long enough for them to fight their way out was a woman, and she had some attitude. Giving her a grin he knew she couldn't see, he said, "Hi, I'm Leon Shield. I'm a Squad Leader in Bravo Company, and I was also the guy who was getting his head cut off."

Lexie didn't appear to hear him and she continued to complain, "Donna, give me the visor. I wanna talk to Ark. Does he know I'm okay?"

Looking over Lexie's shoulder at him, Donna said, "She can't see you, and her hearing isn't great when she comes off the comms gear. If you want to talk to her, then you should touch her arm."

He moved closer to Lexie, and while he touched her arm gently, he repeated, "I'm Leon Shield, Squad Leader in Bravo Company." Lexie seemed to flinch slightly at his touch, and then she slapped his arm. Frowning, he said amiably, "That's an odd response. And I thought you couldn't see."

"I can see shapes," she replied dourly. "And you deserve to be slapped around after the way you treated me." Slapping him again, she said irritably, "There's a person inside that armor, and being thrown around like a sack of dirt isn't any fun for me."

Looking at her slim and leanly muscled body, he decided had he known their Navigator was a woman he probably would have been more considerate. Touching her arm gently again, he said, "Sorry."

Sniffing unhappily, she replied, "You should be." With a slight shrug of her shoulders, she said in a mock sulky tone, "Next time I might let them cut your head off."

Shaking his head, he grinned. "Welcome to Bravo Company."

Donna was wrapping a blanket around Lexie's shoulders, and she looked across at him again. "I'm guessing you haven't heard."

"Heard what?" He asked.

"There's been an emergency recall. We're all going home."

CHAPTER SEVEN:
Homeward bound
(Steve)

A body landed at his feet with a wet thud. The woman had exploded on impact and her face was flattened into the sidewalk. Blood was leaking thickly from her head and torso, but she wasn't one of his so he didn't care, and he stepped over her corpse. Continuing to walk down the street, the screaming and gunfire was louder, but there were far fewer sirens. A man ran towards him brandishing a baseball bat, and then stopped directly in front of him. The end of the bat was sodden with blood and he assumed it had been well used.

With a shock of dark hair flopping over his eyes, the man was covered in blood and none of it was his, but he didn't know how he knew that. While they stood studying one another, the man began to scratch vigorously at his scalp. It reminded him of his own annoying tingling, and he used the gun to dig into his back again. While they stood on the sidewalk facing one another and scratching in unison, people continued to run along the road, and cars were driving erratically around them.

The man was tearing into his scalp so aggressively a chunk of flesh and hair came away from his head. Holding it out like a hairy offering, the man sighed contentedly.

Reaching his other hand to the back of his own head, he dug his nails deep into his scalp, ripping at the already broken skin. The scalp began to peel away under his fingers, and he awkwardly caught the edge until he could pull it away from his skull. It didn't hurt, but the noise inside his head reminded him of ripping Velcro apart. His blood made a warm trail down the back of his neck, and tugging sharply, a chunk of his own hair and skin came away under his fingers. Amused by the effect, he held it out to show the man.

While they stood holding out pieces of themselves to one another, a woman stopped running to stare at them in horror. "What are you doing?"

He was getting rid of his itch once and for all, but he didn't have to tell her that. When he took his hand with the gun from the center of his back, the woman's eyes widened in fear. Without taking her eyes from the weapon, she began to back away. "Please don't shoot me. I can just go. You don't have to kill me."

She didn't belong here anymore than Lucy had and clearly the other man agreed. While she continued to stare at him, the man quickly stepped closer to the woman, and swung his bloodied bat at her head. It connected with the side of her skull with a heavy thud, and she clutched at her face and began to wail. Her outburst didn't deter the man, and he swung again, bringing the woman to her knees. He repeatedly hammered the bat down onto her bent head, beating her to the ground. Each blow was stronger than the last, and eventually the bat snapped with a sharp crack.

"That's not a good weapon," he said flatly.

The end of the bat was hanging by a small piece of splintered wood, and the man studied it dispassionately. Together they began to walk along the sidewalk. Around them vehicles were caught in deep snarls, unable to move and clearly abandoned by their owners. The roads were becoming deeply congested, and more people were running along the cluttered sidewalks. While he and the man kept a steady and calm pace, another man joined them, falling into step as if they'd always walked together. It was a long road, and he and Lucy had often travelled it to visit her parents in Parkway, so he knew it would lead them outside the city.

Albuquerque was a tidy city, filled with modern buildings and wide roads. The city center wasn't huge, but it boasted neat parks, office plazas, swanky hotels, theaters, schools and nightclubs. The region had a long Native American history and was most famous for the Rio Grande River. He hadn't been born in the area, but had settled there with his previous wife. When he'd first moved to Albuquerque, he'd tried their hot air balloon rides and ridden the cable car, and after their divorce, she'd left and he'd stayed. He'd liked having all the benefits of a big city without the congestion.

There were cars parked haphazardly along the wide road, dead bodies were strewn awkwardly, and the city had lost its usually calm atmosphere. Above him were tall buildings and he knew there were more people hiding deep inside them. Some people were being chased along the street, and he could hear the cries of the dying from every direction. None of it bothered him. It was simply their time to leave, and he didn't break his pace or allow himself to become distracted.

By the time he'd reached the interstate, I-40, hundreds of people had joined them on their long march out of the city. Each person was covered in blood that didn't belong to them, and they all carried a weapon of some sort. They marched down the I-40 until there were more than a thousand people following them. Passing by the old town, several thousand more people joined their group. They were a parade of bloodied and silent followers, walking at a steady clip, and ignoring the chaos around them.

He was still wearing his watch, and he noted it had only been three hours since the terrified news reporter had first announced the city was under siege by its own residents. For some reason, he thought he was making good progress, but he didn't know where he was going. His feet seemed to have a mind of their own and they knew where he needed to be. Without looking at his followers, he was aware they were marching in step with one another. They were a single mind with one purpose.

The further they travelled along the I-40, the more people continued to join them, and anyone who didn't understand them ran away when they saw them coming. If they didn't run fast enough, then the followers would kill them, and they were leaving a trail of corpses in their wake. The sound of thousands of feet marching in unison preceded their arrival, and no one challenged them until a Chevrolet Malibu stopped on the road in front of them.

A large man climbed out the vehicle and pointed his gun at him. "Woah, folks, where are you going?"

When he stopped, so did his parade and he studied the man coldly. "I don't know."

"Okay. I'm Sergeant Harry Jones and I'm with Northwest Area Command. The city is under Martial

Law. You folks should go home and wait for the all clear."

His followers were lined up next to him on his left and his right, creating a defiant wall of bodies. "We are going home."

"What do you mean? Where do you live?"

A name popped into his head and he replied, "Near Pueblo Pintado."

"But there's nothing out there. It's a desert. Almost no one lives there."

"We live there."

"Since when."

"Since forever."

The heavyset man looked at him quizzically. What remained of his scalp was still itching, and he reached both hands to his forehead. Digging his nails into his hairline, he scratched and dug into his scalp, tearing at the flesh. It didn't hurt, but blood was running down his forehead and over his eyes. Forgetting about the burly man, he continued to rip at his skin, until he was finally able to grasp the slippery thin flesh between his thumb and forefinger.

"What the hell are you doing?" The large man asked in horror. With a quick glance at his car, he added, "Jas, stay in the car."

Caught up in the pleasure of relieving the itch that had been aggravating him for hours, he ignored the man and peeled the skin down his face. Muscle tore away from his skull and blood ran down his fingers. It was like removing an irritatingly itchy sweater and the relief was immense.

The man was still aiming his weapon at him, but now he was stepping backwards towards his open car door. "You should all stop that. It's not sane," the man said uncertainly.

He didn't care what the man thought, he didn't belong here anymore than Lucy did. Tearing the last of his face from his neck, he held the loose flap of skin in his hand. He didn't need it anymore, and he tossed it to the ground where it landed with a graceless flop onto the asphalt in front of him. Running his bloodied hands over his exposed skull, it didn't have the bone structure he expected, and he looked at the man next to him. Instead of a white skull, the man's face was a hardened shell with humanoid features, only it was black and rubbery looking.

While the heavy man climbed into his vehicle, he tried to smile at the man next to him, but his face didn't move that way anymore. The fine slit that represented his mouth didn't change, and he poked his finger at his nose, only to find he no longer had holes where his nostrils should be. His face was a hardened mask, and if he looked anything like the man next to him, he no longer had eyeballs, only dark round circles with no iris or color.

The vehicle was reversing away from him and his followers, and it quickly accelerated, heading out of the city in the direction he planned to go. His arm was itchy, so he shrugged his coat off and began to dig at his forearm. Like the skin on his face, he no longer felt bone under his flesh. His skin was covering something else, and continuing to attack his arm, he pierced the skin until he was able to tear it away. A hardened blackness appeared under the ripped skin on his arm. Rubbing it aggressively, it revealed a rubbery, black and slightly shiny surface. While he pulled at the flesh on his forearm, his fingers began to slough away, and a thin black hand with knobbly joints appeared.

All around him his followers were copying his actions, and soon the street was littered with slabs of human skin and abandoned clothes.

CHAPTER EIGHT:
Step up or out
(Jonesy)

"What the fuck was that?" Jas asked, but the shudder in her voice betrayed her fear.

The man had torn off his own face. Someone attacking themselves that way wasn't outside the realms of what was possible, but it usually involved drugs or severe mental illness. The real strangeness wasn't the apparent self-mutilation, but what was underneath the skin. The pitch black, rubbery looking face wasn't human, and if he hadn't seen it with his own eyes, he wouldn't have believed it.

"I dunno."

"B...b...but there were thousands of them. They were all doing it. What are they?"

He wasn't sure what they were, but he was confident they were the reason the city had collapsed. He and Jas had been driving for half an hour and it was a complete waste of time. The streets were jammed with abandoned cars, injured people and lunatics. He'd witnessed citizens being attacked, but there was nothing they could do about it. They'd been making their way across the city to his apartment to find Jenny, when they'd run across the swarm of people walking along the I-40.

Jas had been trying to stay in contact with dispatch, but the comms line was flaky and she couldn't always get through. Even when she did, they had nothing new to tell her, but what they'd just witnessed was important and he needed to tell Jo.

The radio crackled and he heard the dispatcher. "This is dispatch. Who am I talking to?"

His car didn't have a standard police radio and Jas was using the mike attached to her uniform. Stretching his arm across her chest, he said, "Gimme the radio." When Jas pulled it from her shirt and handed it to him, he said, "This is Harry Jones and I need to speak to the Commander urgently."

"Sorry, but the best I can do is pass a message onto her."

"Not good enough. She needs to know what I've seen."

The operator hesitated, then he heard the sound of the line being transferred, and Jo's voice came on the radio. "Jonesy?"

"Yeah."

"What is it? Make it quick. The lines aren't stable and I could lose you."

"I just saw something very weird. There's about thirty thousand people leaving the city via the Interstate."

"I don't blame them for leaving."

"That's not the point. They started tearing their faces off and underneath there was…some sort of rubbery, black looking humanoid face."

Jo didn't reply immediately and then she asked, "Are you sure?"

"Err, yeah, I saw it with my own eyes."

She hesitated again. "I need to put the city under Martial Law, but I'm not sure how. We've lost track of most of the officers, and I don't think the Army or National Guard are coming."

"What does that mean?"

"I think it means it's every man for himself. We don't have the ability to establish control over the situation."

"Are you saying the city has fallen in three hours?"

"I think so, but I've never been in this situation before. In every disaster scenario we assumed a much slower rate of collapse. We never anticipated how to deal with what looks like half the population attacking one another randomly. There's no logic to this. We don't know who will become an attacker and who will be their victim. We don't know even know who to protect, and none of our forces are immune." Jo lowered her voice and added, "I don't even know if you and I are immune. It's possible the person next to you right now could try and kill you for no reason."

The implications of her words were slowly sinking in. There was no government control left in place, and the country was effectively falling, but to what? The people he'd watched tear themselves apart weren't human. Based on what they looked like on the surface, they had once been human, but he wasn't sure what they were becoming.

"Is it a virus?" He asked.

"I don't know and I don't think it matters either. We are where we are, and I don't have anyone left."

"What are your orders?"

"I'm not sure I've got any or anyone left to give them to."

He could hear the confusion in her words and her voice. They hadn't planned for a situation where the population turned against one another in such an unpredictable or complete way. Having witnessed the mob leaving the city, it was obvious something had changed them. One minute they'd looked like regular people, and then they'd turned into something completely alien. If they'd just turned without doing anyone any harm, then he would have assumed they were sick and needed help. It wasn't the change that was causing the problem, but the fact they were murdering people for no reason. That changed the nature of the situation from people becoming ill to an assault on the city.

"Do you think we're under attack?"

"What do you mean?" Jo asked.

"Is this some sort of takeover? You know, like a terrorist attack?"

"I don't think anyone could convince regular people to start killing their families like this on such a wide scale basis at the same time."

He agreed no conventional enemy could do that, but what if there was another enemy? An enemy they didn't know they had. What if this was some sort of alien attack?

"What if we have an enemy we don't know about? I mean, those people I saw didn't look human anymore. What if they're not? What if we've been invaded in some way and didn't know it?"

"Do you think this is an invasion?"

Staring through his windshield, all he could see were crashed cars and fires burning on the street and in the buildings. A woman clutching a child ran from a door and disappeared into an alley. If he wound down his window, he would clearly hear gunfire and screaming. He peered up at the windows above the road where a man was fighting with a woman on a small balcony. It would remain to be seen which of them would plummet to the ground. There wasn't anything he could do about it, and within moments it was the woman who fell. She landed only fifty yards away from him, and she clumsily clambered to her feet and ran back into the building. Her hard landing hadn't even left her stunned.

"It looks like an invasion out here. And it doesn't matter if it is an invasion or not, we need to assume it is."

Jo spoke again, only now her tone was decisive. "Okay. Okay. I get what you're saying. If this is an invasion, then we need to regroup."

Being side-lined and preparing to retire, he'd never had much to do with Jo. She was the Commander of the Northwest Area Command and he was only a Sergeant. Most people had spoken highly of her and he'd had no reason to think any differently. He waited to find out just how smart Jo really was and she didn't disappoint him.

Her voice came over the radio again. "We need to direct people to a safe place. Somewhere we can regroup and prepare to fight against whatever this is."

"Where?" Jo didn't answer and he worried they'd lost the line. "Jo, are you still there?"

"Yes. I'm looking at map. I think the best place to send people is Kirtland Air Force Base. It's only a few miles from the city. Spread the word, Jonesy, and I'll get the message out in every way I can."

"Will you go there too?"

This time she hesitated for longer. "No, my job is to protect the city, and the best thing I can do is get everyone to head to the base, but you go there and tell them what you saw."

He didn't really know Jo, but his instinct was to tell her to leave and go somewhere safe. Hesitating himself, he thought about Jenny and their daughter, Miranda. She'd moved to Las Vegas with her husband, Darren, and he should get Jenny and then look for her. She was four months pregnant with their first grandchild and she was his primary responsibility. Being so close to retirement, he'd sort of forgotten about being a cop, but Jo was right, it was still his job.

"I...I need to find my family, Jo."

"I appreciate your position, but you're a cop first and that means you need to take care of the people."

"I'm only half a mile from my apartment. I need to get my wife and then go to Las Vegas to find my daughter. She's pregnant."

"I understand. Get your wife and then go to the base. Hopefully there'll be people there that can help you find your daughter."

Her orders didn't make him happy and a part of him wanted to ignore her. Under their current circumstances she couldn't make him do anything.

"Jonesy," she said sternly. "You have information and you might be the only one who knows it. Step up. Your record is impeccable. Don't screw it up at the last minute. You're a good cop, so go be one."

He knew his record was perfect, but in his view it wasn't much of an achievement. He'd turned up to work, done his job diligently, and kept his nose clean. It didn't make him a great cop, only a man who did his job professionally. He wasn't even trying to be professional, that was a by-product of following the rules. With a slow dawning awareness, he realized his commitment to his job had never really been tested. Now he was being asked to choose. Would he take care of his own interests first, or would he serve and protect? Before he had a chance to speak, the line went dead.

CHAPTER NINE:
Graduation Day
(Dayton)

The crawlspace in the ceiling of the hospital was dusty and cramped. He wasn't even supposed to be at work today, but after watching the news he'd felt compelled to head straight to the emergency room. On his way to the hospital, he'd witnessed more gunfire and assaults than he'd ever seen in any movie and the room below him was a testimony to the murders taking place on the streets.

"What do we do now?" The woman whispered urgently.

Her face was gloomily lit through the cracks in the ceiling tiles and he held his finger to his lips. Peering through the small gap, he adjusted his position on the supporting beam he was lying on. Below them was a small hospital ward with four beds. Every bed was covered in blood, and the motionless bodies were lying awkwardly on their narrow cots. When he'd walked into the room the fire alarm had begun its irritating whooping sound, and people were running wildly through the corridors outside. Noticing the red stains on the pale blue blankets on the beds, he'd quickly flicked each one back, only to discover every patient had been repeatedly stabbed. After a quick check that they were dead, he'd turned to leave the room and collided with the woman he was now with.

It was then he'd heard the gunfire, and they'd piled a chair onto a bureau in the room and clambered into the ceiling. If he hadn't witnessed the violence on the streets, he might have thought he was being overcautious, but within seconds of replacing the ceiling tile, someone had opened rapid fire into the room below them. The shooter was a middle-aged man wearing jeans and a leather jacket. He was now walking between the beds, checking each occupant, and peering under the metal cots. The chair they'd used to climb into the ceiling was now lying on the floor and the man eyed it suspiciously.

"Is there anyone here?"

The woman was lying along the beam in front of him, and their heads were so close they were almost touching. A dusty web swung slowly in the bright beam of light. He could hear her panicked breathing, and reached out a hand to touch her shoulder. If the large man holding the semi-automatic weapon suspected they were there, then it would be easy for him to fire into the ceiling. With only the thin tiles between them, the bullets would rip through the fabric and into their prone bodies.

While he breathed shallowly, a woman walked into the room. To his surprise, the man didn't shoot her and said, "It's empty."

"But I saw one of them come in here," she replied disdainfully.

"You couldn't have. There's no one here."

Walking across the small room, the woman peered out of the window to the ground three floors below. "Well, she didn't leave through the window. There's no way down."

"Why are you being stubborn? If she's not here, she's not here."

"I'm not being stubborn. I just know what I saw."

The brutish looking man stared at the woman blankly and then seemed to come to a decision. "We're wasting time. We have to leave soon, and we should kill as many as we can before we go." Even as he spoke, he was already striding from the room.

Watching him leave, the woman frowned to herself and began to inspect the bodies lying on their beds. "I know you're in here. You won't get away from me."

The ward below them was for terminal patients, mostly suffering from late stage cancer. Each one was dressed in their pajamas, and they were thin to the point of being skeletal. He suspected their untimely deaths had come less than a week before their diseases would have claimed them. Although they'd been destined to die soon, they didn't deserve to be murdered or cheated of their last days on earth. He felt resentful on their behalf, and narrowed his eyes at the woman still prodding their silent corpses. A familiar anger was building up in him, and he wanted take revenge for the lost lives lying below him. Whoever these killers were, they had no right to prey on the vulnerable, and the people they'd murdered deserved to be cared for, not violently attacked.

Quietly fumbling in his shirt pocket, his fingers felt the sharp end of his gold ballpoint pen. It was a graduation gift from his father, not for becoming a doctor, but for his final year at high school. His father hadn't even lived long enough to see him graduate from school, and he'd handed it to him while he lay dying of cancer. Remembering his father, the deaths of the people in the beds felt personal, and his anger was turning into a white rage. His father had stipulated his life insurance be set aside to pay for his education, and he'd chosen to specialize in Oncology in his honor.

The woman below him was wearing scrubs and he assumed she worked at the hospital. Obviously still puzzled by where the woman with him had gone, she was standing with her back to him and staring out of the door. Angling his head against the beam, he looked over the woman's head at the people still moving through the corridor. They'd lost their panicked air, and seemed to walking with purpose towards the elevators at the end of the corridor. Although there was still sporadic gunfire from various levels of the hospital, the sound had diminished considerably. It was a good-sized hospital, with at least a thousand patients and fifteen fully functioning operating theatres. Having its own trauma center, it was able to take in emergency cases, and it had been overflowing with people when he'd arrived. The reception area had been standing room only, and some patients were being treated for injuries in the corridors. He estimated there'd been at least four thousand people inside and around the hospital.

While he waited for the woman to make up her mind to stay or leave, the hospital was falling strangely silent. Just as he was thinking she might leave, the woman hiding in the ceiling with him sneezed. The effect was immediate, and the woman below spun and stared up at the ceiling accusingly. He didn't wait to see what she would do, but allowed his body to roll from the beam and onto the thin tiles. Working long hours on stressful cancer cases left him little time to eat well or work out, and his hefty two hundred and fifty pound body shattered the ceiling tiles underneath him.

The body of one of the deceased cancer patients broke his fall with an ugly squelch, and he silently thanked them for their one last service to mankind. One of the advantages of being a large six foot three man who never found time for the gym, was he had a good amount of padding. His generous rump and well-covered belly took the brunt of the impact, and he felt the crunch of bones snapping beneath him. He was surprisingly agile for his size and less than average fitness, and he bounced from the bed landing on his feet. Without stopping his momentum, he crashed into the scrub-wearing nurse, hammering her against the wall.

The woman was clawing at his face and he was surprised at the strength of her fingers. He grabbed at the hand reaching for his eyes and snapped her fingers back, only they bent in an unnatural way, and her forefinger touched the back of her wrist. She should have screamed in pain, but she made no sound and ripped at his face with her other hand.

"Open the window!" He shouted, hoping the other woman would hear him.

Ignoring the pain in his face, he pulled his father's pen from his pocket and jabbed it into the woman's gut. It should have been sharp enough to penetrate, but it simply slid over her belly. She was incredibly strong, and in desperation, he let go of her hand and grabbed at her mid-length blonde hair. Clutching a fistful, he tried to haul her away from the wall towards the window. He felt her scalp give under his tight grip, and half of her face pulled away from her skull. It should have been enough to stop her, but it didn't, and under her face the flesh was black and rubbery looking.

The woman had recovered from his attack, and with her hand now free, she grabbed him by the throat. He pulled away from her grip, but she tightened it and followed his movement. He could feel her fingers digging deeply into his throat and he punched at her wildly. Her body was jerking and he couldn't work out why. Opening his eyes fully, he stared over the head of his attacker at the other woman, who was now heaving a chair repeatedly at the woman's back. Being hit was a force that should have at least distracted her, his attacker continued to clutch his throat, but each blow was pushing her closer to him.

With her near enough to him, he grabbed her shoulders, and pulled her into a tight bear hug. At that angle, she was forced to loosen her grip around his throat. The other woman had turned her assault with the chair onto the window, and was slamming it hard against the glass. It was safety glass so it didn't break, but small cracks appeared. Still holding the woman to him in a tight hug, he used his extra weight against her, pushing her towards the window. With a fast heave of his arms, he slammed the woman against the window, and the glass shattered. She bulged outward until her spine was bent ninety degrees over the windowsill, and she was finally forced to let go of his throat, but he felt his flesh give.

The woman was howling and she sounded outraged and angry. With her head hanging outside of the window, very little of her cries could be heard inside the room. He and the other woman looked at one another, and then without saying a word, they each grabbed one of the woman's legs and flipped her over the windowsill. In unison, they followed the move by peering over the edge and watching the woman fall the three stories to the ground. She landed awkwardly, but climbed to her feet and glared up at them angrily.

The woman turned to him in disbelief. "What the hell…?"

Having seen the blackness under the woman's skin, and felt her almost mechanical fingers digging into his throat, he was unsurprised she'd landed so well. Nothing about the woman had reminded him of anything human. When he turned to stare through the door, people were still making their way along the corridor, only now some were looking into their room curiously. Given they weren't attacking one another, he thought it was safe to assume they were all like the woman they'd just thrown from the window. It would only be a matter of seconds before they realized they weren't one of them.

"We have to go."

Without waiting for an answer, he grabbed the woman by the arm and ran from the room, turning in the opposite direction to the elevators and public stairwell. The hospital had been custom built, and on the other side of the building were staff stairs and a service elevator. Skirting the walls of the corridor, he rapidly made his way along it, heading for the rear of the hospital. People were brushing past him, and when he glanced into each room he passed, all he saw were bodies and blood. Travelling in the opposite direction to everyone else, they were gaining more attention, and it would only be moments before they were discovered. Some of the people were wearing scrubs, others were casually dressed, and even more were clad in their pajamas. The oddest sight he witnessed was a man, still naked, with his entire chest exposed. Instead of a smooth chest, the man had a black, rubbery hole where his heart should have been.

Pushing open a door on his left, he dragged the woman into the room behind him. Turning abruptly, he slammed the hydraulic door closed as quickly as it would shut. Next to the door was a heavy set of cabinets on wheels, which he pushed it in front of it. Kicking the wheels sharply, he felt his big toe break, but he continued to hammer at the wheel until it snapped and the cabinet drooped on one side. The woman copied him, and together they broke the wheel on the other side. It wouldn't hold the door for long, and he grabbed the woman again, pulling her towards the next set of doors.

The next room was another ward, only this one was larger. With twelve beds, six on each side, he dragged the woman through the aisle down the center, and tried to ignore the bloodied beds.

"What's going on?" The woman asked breathlessly.

He couldn't answer that question, other than to say people had gone completely insane, and appeared to be turning into rubbery monsters, intent on killing everyone. It didn't strike him as a sane answer, and he didn't have the breath to spare so he didn't reply. He needed to get to the service elevators. Not the ones they used for visitors or even the extra-large ones they used for surgery. Originally, the hospital had been funded by a very wealthy man who'd insisted on having a top floor office. Given he'd donated all the money to build and run the hospital, when he'd asked for his own private elevator, the architects had simply added one to the plans. Their crazy benefactor was long gone and, with the endless budget cuts over the years, the elevator was no longer used or maintained. Their only hope was to find that elevator and ride their way to freedom. The hospital was lost. All of his patients had either turned into killers or had been murdered.

In all the years he'd practiced, he'd never given up on a patient no matter how terminal their case, and he wasn't about to give up on himself either.

CHAPTER TEN:
Home Sweet Home
(Leon)

The recall had been abrupt and uninformative. Judging by the long queues at every military base they landed at, absolutely everyone was being called home, but no one had offered an explanation as to why. To his surprise, every airport was under heavy security, and not a single television was working. He'd tried his mobile phone continuously and got no signal. Clustered together in groups of dusty, camouflaged sandy brown, they'd all guessed about what was happening, but no one had any real information.

The mass exodus was being done in any way possible, and now he was sitting in a C-5 Galaxy transport plane with hundreds of other troopers. They still had their packs and guns, and were leaning on one another for support while they tried to sleep. Unlike a typical military flight, everything inside the plane had been ditched to make room for people, and many were lying on the floor, using one another and their woobies as pillows. Leaning back in his narrow seat against the side of the plane, his own lightweight poncho lining was tucked behind his head. From the rumors he'd heard, all of the ships had been loaded with more troops and were heading home. Another story he'd heard was all commercial flights had been grounded and only the military were using the airspace.

There must have been two hundred and fifty men and women in the belly of the transport plane, and he was sitting in a line with Tuck, Billy, Donna and their ill-tempered Navigator, Lexie. With food and coffee, she seemed to have recovered from her ordeal, and while he gingerly fingered the knife wound on his neck, he couldn't fault her commitment. She'd saved their lives and he supposed she was entitled to a small tantrum, if only as tension relief from a tough situation that could have killed them all.

He had no idea how close they were to landing, but they'd been flying for hours. The transport plane had a top speed of five hundred and eighty miles per hour, and it was a long flight home. At first he'd been tired, but now he was bored and idly flicking through the pictures on his camera. In one picture, Amelia was smiling at him. Her face was framed by a poufy veil, and her lips were a bright red in stark contrast to her white dress.

"What's that?" Lexie asked loudly in his ear.

With the droning of the plane, he could hardly hear her and shouted back, "Amelia. My wife. She's pregnant. Our baby's due in four months."

Lexie was dressed in her under gear including her hydraulics, but her armor was piled at her feet and she was using it as a footrest. His face reflected at him through the visor covering half of her face and he decided, despite sleeping most of the flight, he still looked tired. The past eight years had aged him, but he couldn't work out if he'd developed lines due to what he'd seen, or his body had simply leaned down with age and fitness. Gone was his rounded face, and it had been replaced by a chiseled jawline topped with deep-set hazel eyes. The corners of his mouth had developed deep creases, and his cheekbones were slightly hollowed. He'd long given up any attempt to control his hair, and it was shorn close to his scalp. One of his incisors had been chipped by the recoil of an M4, and he thought he should get it fixed, but he didn't really want to waste the money. He suspected Amelia would think differently, and he'd find himself at the dentist the moment she got her hands on him. Thinking about Amelia reminded him he was soon to be a father, and he continued flicking through the pictures on his phone.

"What's that?" Lexie asked again.

On his phone was a picture of him and Amelia at San Juan Island, and he replied, "Our honeymoon. We only got married three months ago. She was two months pregnant."

Lexie didn't reply and he looked at her quizzically, but instead of seeing his reflection in her visor, she was looking at someone at the front of the plane. Glancing to his right, he tried to see what she was looking at. Seeing nothing other than a clump of troopers lying on the floor, he asked, "What are you looking at?"

With only her mouth and nose on display, he couldn't read her expression and she pointed. "That guy. The one at the back."

"Why?"

"His read is funny."

"Like funny ha ha or funny weird."

"That's a stupid question," she replied bluntly. "His signal isn't right."

Turning to face Donna sitting next to her, she seemed to disappear into a conversation with her. Obviously she was done talking to him, and he continued to flick through the hundreds of images on his phone. He was excited about going home. Usually they were deployed for up to twelve months, and he'd prepared himself for the worst case scenario where he'd miss the pregnancy, birth and first six months of his son's life. Being recalled was an unexpected bonus and, despite the strangeness of their situation, he was looking forward to surprising Amelia. She'd gotten pregnant within a week of them meeting and it was a shotgun wedding. He was excited about becoming a father, but he wanted to spend some uninterrupted time with Amelia. They didn't really know one another, and swept up with the idea of becoming a father, he'd married her hoping it would all work out in the end. It wasn't a good way to start their lives and his parents weren't happy.

With the loud droning of the plane it took him a while to realize something was happening at the front. It was only when the people at his feet began to rise from the floor that he looked up. There seemed to be some sort of argument going on at the front of the plane, and soldiers were piling on top of one another.

"Do not fire!" A voice roared.

The order was relayed around the cramped plane and more people were moving to the back. As soldiers scrambled away, the fight at the front was becoming an isolated area of its own. Dragging men and women out of combat, and then dumping them into an emergency recall, was a sure fire way to stress them out. It didn't surprise him that some people were losing their cool, but the panicked movement in front of him seemed to be an overreaction to a simple brawl. He looked around for his

CO, or at least someone senior, only to realize he was the one in the middle of the fight. No one was throwing any punches, and the group of ten or so men appeared to have someone pinned to the floor.

"What the fuck are they doing?" Tuck asked in a disgruntled tone.

He was about to say he didn't know, when another soldier approached the free-for-all, and jabbed his fist into the spine of a man lying on top. Assuming he'd landed his punch, he was surprised when the man then lifted the other man from the top of the pack. He must have been holding onto his spine, and the other man lifted into the air briefly, until his bodyweight dragged him down again, leaving the man with a part of the spine in his hand. Without thinking, he dropped his phone and grabbed for his gun.

"What the fuck...!"

"Do not fire! Do not fire!"

The order echoed from person to person, and he dropped his gun again, reaching for his knife as he did. A surge of bodies hit him from his right, and he was pushed along with them to the back of the plane. Unable to see anything other than the people around him, he grabbed the webbing on the wall behind the row of chairs, and hauled himself up until he was standing on a seat. From his higher vantage point, he watched the escalating fight at the front of the plane. The man who'd torn the spine out of the other man was now falling under the bodies and knives of more soldiers. Where he would have expected the man to collapse, he didn't and he was tearing into his assailants with his bare hands. Clearly their blood was flowing, and the floor of the plane was growing red and slippery. Directly in front of him a man began to assault the soldier next to him. This one was using his knife to good effect, and bodies were falling around him. Still holding onto the webbing, he lashed at out the man with his blade, slicing him across the cheek. Instead of sinking into his flesh, the knife skidded across the surface of the man's face. Tuck was standing on a chair beside him, and he used the butt of his M4 to smash the top of the man's head. Both attacks had no effect, and the man continued to stab at the people around him. Blood was spilling and draining into the grills on the floor, and people were sliding and falling.

The central area of the plane erupted into violence, and all he could see were blades and bodies slamming into one another. He wanted to help, but it was impossible to work out who was attacking who. The floor was a sea of violent movement, and while he watched in shock, their Navigator stood up in front of him. Without much regard for either side, Lexie appeared in full armor and began to push bodies aside as she targeted a soldier. With a swift motion, she grabbed the man, flipped him on his stomach and held him down. Seeing her actions, other soldiers grabbed at the man and kept him pinned to the floor.

Realizing they needed to secure the manic soldiers, he began to pull at the webbing on the wall. It wasn't designed to hold anyone, but he figured it could be used like a net. Lexie reached for another man, and grabbing him by the neck, she hurled him roughly at the front of the plane. With the strength of her hydraulics, the man flew through the air and landed against the bulkhead, sliding down and then bouncing to his feet. With the force of his impact against the wall, it wasn't possible for the man to have felt nothing, and yet he was already up again and ready to assault another person.

He, Tuck and Billy, along with others, were tearing the netting from the wall. Without a word being spoken, other soldiers grabbed at the netting, clearly understanding their plan. With Lexie throwing the now enemy soldiers at the front of the plane, they gradually used the netting to form a barrier between them. Lexie was continuing to target soldiers in the crowd, and slowly a line of killers and defenders was forming. The front of the plane became the killers and the back the defenders. It was a life and death football match and the losers would die.

"We're trapped. They've gotta land," a voice shouted desperately in his ear.

The line of defenders cut across the plane, and they were hammering the butts of their guns into the netting. The killer soldiers were being pushed into the wall at the front of the plane. There were bodies lying prone across the floor, and people were clambering over them as if they weren't there. At least a hundred men and women were now caught behind the netting, but it didn't stop them and it offered no protection. The only thing keeping them alive was the relentless battering of fists and guns against the front of the crowd. They wouldn't be able hold their impossible perimeter for long, before the killers would burst through the netting and the plane would erupt into hopeless violence.

Lexie was at the front of the plane adding her hydraulic strength to the battle. Thanks to the hydraulics, her blows were having more effect, but she was only one person against a hundred. The netting, which was a fairly useless defense from the start, was being torn away and some of the killers were emerging from the fray. Their faces were battered and torn, and under the bloodied mess, all he could see was a rubbery blackness.

It was only then he realized the plane was descending rapidly, but it was unsteady. As the plane rocked from side to side, everyone was being thrown around. With the netting gone from the wall, he had nothing to hold onto and was hurled into the sea of living and dead bodies. Rushing air was filling the large transport space, and the rear door was lowering. Obviously the pilot had decided it was better they fall to their deaths than die inside the cramped space. Struggling to his feet, and pushing himself against the bodies pressing on him, he stared towards the opening door. Caught in the fight, he hadn't noticed their fast descent, and the ground was closer than he expected.

He clearly wasn't the only one who understood what that meant, and behind him was the distinct crack of gunfire. They were firing on their own, but what choice did they have? The large door was almost fully extended, and with the sharp descent of the plane, he felt himself sliding towards it. Grappling with the floor and bodies around him, he tried to control his tumbling. There was no way he wasn't going to fall out of the plane, but every second he managed to delay it would bring him closer to the ground. There was nothing to hold onto, and he tipped onto his back trying to minimize the damage, as he slid with everyone else towards the gaping door.

It was only as his body left the platform that he felt something grab hold of his belt. Fighting against the fierce wind whipping at his face, he saw a black arm and Lexie holding onto the edge of the door. Bodies were flying past him, bouncing onto the tarmac and skidding to a stop. Finally, the wheels of the transport plane hit solid ground and it began to lose speed.

CHAPTER ELEVEN:
Until death do us part
(Jonesy)

His apartment block was old and only four-stories high. When they'd married, Jenny's father had helped them put a small deposit on the property and they'd long since paid it off. They'd lived on the third floor for thirty years, and unlike modern apartments, it had a balcony and generous sized rooms with high ceilings. Although they'd often talked about moving to the suburbs, the city was both his job and his home. They'd lived a simple life, and having always watched their money, he could retire early without having to take another job. He and Jenny had planned to enjoy living in downtown Albuquerque, but he guessed that idea was all blown to hell now.

Turning to Jas, he said, "You can stay in the car or come with me, but either way it isn't safe."

She'd said very little during their drive across the city, but he'd noticed she made good decisions. Even now, she'd parked the car as close to the entrance as she could without compromising their ability to leave quickly. When they'd witnessed the mob tearing their faces off, she hadn't panicked and had driven away at a sensible speed.

"I'll come with you."

He'd armed them with an AR-15 and a shotgun from the trunk of his car, but neither of them were wearing bulletproof vests. Usually they were supplied by the precinct, and they weren't something he'd ever thought to buy. Glancing through the windshield, he tried to assess the risks around them. Their apartment wasn't on a main road, and they were parked on one of the narrower side streets. Cars had been abandoned along the sidewalks, and smoke was billowing from a window to his left. A lost dog was wandering down the road, and it stopped and nosed at a corpse half lying outside the passenger door of a car. He'd never been to a war zone, but he supposed this is what it would look like. Without the hustle and bustle of city life, the area had already taken on a dusty and abandoned look.

To his right were the heavy doors that led into his apartment block. Every level had four homes, and the whole complex had fourteen apartments. Unlike some of the modern apartment blocks, there was no doorman or reception, and only a wide set of stairs leading to each level. The double front doors had been painted a thick, dark brown, and one of them was slightly ajar, meaning it wasn't locked. Usually the janitor only locked the doors at night, and he wasn't surprised to see they were open. He supposed they should have been more security conscious, but nothing bad had ever happened on their street.

"Let's do this," he said tersely.

They made their way up the short flight of stairs to the open door, and he listened closely for any sounds. The street was worryingly quiet, and other than some distant gunfire, he heard nothing. Jas eased the door open while he trained his weapon at the gloomy darkness inside. He half-expected Missus Starling from the ground floor to leap out at him. She'd always been an angry woman, and he could easily imagine her turning into a ruthless killer. Despite his concern, there was no movement inside the small entranceway, and he cautiously climbed onto the first step of the landing. It groaned under his weight, reminding him he needed to go on a diet. Dismissing the irrelevant thought, he peered up the stairwell at the long lines of stairs and handrails. Specks of dust were drifting idly in the light from the windows over each set of stairs. Nothing seemed to be disturbed, and he continued to move as quietly as he could up the flight of stairs.

All he could hear was the rustle of Jas's jacket as she followed him, and again he noted her natural instinct for police work. She was at least six feet behind him, not too close and not too far. If they survived the invasion, as he thought of it, he would highly recommend her for keeping such a cool head in a crisis. Reaching the first level, he noticed all of the heavy, dark doors were closed, and the landing was clear. He continued to the next level, only this time he looked out of the clear windows at the city. With the taller buildings around him there wasn't much to see, but he noticed more grey smoke was seeping along the skyline.

On the second floor, once again all of the doors on the landing were closed and he continued to the third floor. Their apartment was next the stairwell, which might have made it noisy, but being a small block with an established occupancy, it had never been an issue. Fumbling the keys from his pant pocket, he prepared to unlock the door. It was an old style double lock that needed two keys. He inserted the heavy brass key into the first lock, flinching at the loud noise it made as the tumblers turned. The second key was smaller and it opened the deadlock. He twisted the key and pushed against the door. As it swung open, a blur of movement caught his eye, and something came through the small opening in a flash of frenzied motion. The small and heavy body hit him squarely in the gut, but with him being so much larger it made little impact. Instinctively he pushed at the body and caught sight of Jenny's face. It was twisted with rage and she snarled at him angrily.

The shock of seeing his wife of over thirty years staring at him with such clear hatred caught him off guard. It wasn't just her expression, but her eyes were black and her hair was falling out in clumps. In her hand she held a small and bloodied knife, and he looked down at his substantial stomach. His usually crisp blue shirt was turning red, and he realized she'd stabbed him. Luckily, there was a good amount of fat between the shirt and his internal organs, and she'd probably done little damage.

Before he could react, Jas opened fire with her AR-15. Just as she'd told him, she was a good shot and every bullet was hitting its mark. The force of her fire was pushing Jenny backwards, and pieces of her flesh were flying into the air. His brain became confused and he roared, "Ceasefire! Stop!"

Jas ignored him and continued to pace forward, firing as she did. Jenny was being pushed further into the apartment, and she finally fell over the well-padded arm of their three-seater sofa. Once Jenny tumbled into the pillows, Jas stood over her and continued to fire. At such close range every bullet should have been a killing one, but Jenny acted as if nothing was happening. She continued to flail against the soft furnishings, trying to sit up and find her feet again. Still wearing her short nightgown, it was bunched around her waist, displaying her full, white panties. Jenny wasn't a small woman, and the bullets were punching holes into her soft belly, but she wasn't bleeding enough for such devastating injuries.

After what seemed like a long time, but was probably less than a minute, Jas's gun clicked empty. It was one of those defining moments in his life. He'd always thought of himself as a reasonable man, and he'd taken the easiest and safest option every time. Jenny had been an unambitious woman, and marrying her had meant she would never push him to do more than he wanted to. Staying with the police force had been an easy way to live. They'd told him what to do and he'd always done as he was told. Even working on the beat had been a fairly safe option. He'd never been ambitious and had left the heroics to others. He was a considered a big, friendly bear of a man who could be relied upon for a joke and a shallow take on the world. Some days he wondered if he'd ever really lived at all, but he always dismissed the thought and got back to doing more and thinking less.

Jenny was staring up at him with her black, empty eyes, and he knew he had to decide what he was going to do. There was no one to tell him what his next step should be. In a crisis the mind works at a stunning speed, and in a cascade of rapid thoughts, he decided the creature in front of him wasn't Jenny. Lifting his shotgun, he aimed and prepared to fire while shouting to Jas, "Run!"

Jas had already reloaded her AR-15 and ignored his order. With her gun ready to fire, she grabbed the back of his shirt and pulled him towards the door. Jenny was still struggling to rise from the sofa and he stepped back with Jas.

"You can't kill it. We need to lock it up," she shouted.

No amount of bullets had taken Jenny down. As her flesh had been blown away from her face and body, all it had revealed was a rubbery blackness. The thing on the sofa was not his wife and it seemed to be impossible to kill. It reminded him of the woman who'd fallen three stories, then got up, and run back into the building. Whatever these things were, they didn't die easily or possibly at all.

They covered the short distance to the door, and seeing the key was still in the deadlock, he pulled it closed. Jenny was clearly on her feet, and she was hammering at the door, howling in frustration. Jas was leaning her back against the window in the stairwell with her head bent, and she was breathing deeply.

Finally looking at him, she said, "That was close."

In a stunned tone that reflected how he was feeling, he replied, "That was my wife."

Through the shock, he felt the dampness around his belly and looked down at himself. Gingerly running his fingers across his shirt, there was a slight indentation where the knife had penetrated.

Watching him, she said firmly, "We need to patch that."

He kept a first aid kit in his car and he was fairly sure the wound was superficial. Nodding, he looked back at the door that continued to emit a muffled banging sound. It had been his home for thirty years, and he remembered painting the door a deep, dark blue. His entire life had been behind that well-painted door, but now it was gone. His wife was effectively dead, and the thing that wanted to kill him wasn't anyone he knew. In the hours they'd spent driving around the city, witnessing the murders and devastation, he'd still believed the situation was retrievable, but now he knew it wasn't. Life as he'd known it had changed forever, and whether he liked it or not, he had to step up.

"We have to go."

"Where to now?" She asked uncertainly.

Jo had told him to get people to Kirtland Air Force Base, and for the first time he was ready to follow his orders. "We need to start looking for survivors and telling them to go to the base."

"Survivors?"

"Yeah, that's what anyone left alive is...a survivor."

"Jonesy?" A voice asked hesitantly.

It was Missus Starling's voice, and he looked up the stairwell at her anxious face. "Missus Starling?"

Her wrinkled face was framed by flyaway white hair and it creased into a shy smile. "Call me Clarissa." Waving her delicate, blue-veined hand at him, she added, "We're all up here on the fourth floor. We've been waiting for help to arrive."

Following her loosely fitting, polyester clad legs up the stairs, she led them into a top floor apartment. There were only two apartments on this level and they were both larger than his own. Inside the generous lounge were seven people, mostly in their fifties and sixties. These were the people who hadn't gone to work that morning, and had stayed secured in their apartments while the city fell apart. Although he wouldn't call any of them friends, he knew them all well enough to speak to.

Doug from the second floor asked, "What's going on?"

Louise from the first floor said, "We banged on your door, but Jenny didn't answer. Is she okay?"

John from the second floor said, "Sorry, but I broke into this apartment figuring it was safer if we all stayed together."

Geoff from the third floor added, "The TV isn't working anymore and neither are the phones...not even the landlines."

Clarissa said, "You're hurt. Let me get you something for that."

They were all eager to talk to him, but he didn't know what to say. Remembering his wife and her attempt to kill him, he knew what he had to do. The city was infiltrated with creatures like Jenny and they needed to leave. It wasn't safe to stay, but he had no idea how he could move seven defenseless people. Guns didn't kill these creatures and he had no way to protect them.

Clarissa had returned with a box of bandages, a damp towel and a tube of antiseptic cream. Sitting heavily in a chair, he allowed her to undo his shirt and wipe at the blood still seeping from the cut.

"Are you okay, Jonesy?"

Finally finding his thoughts and his tongue, he replied, "Yeah. Jenny is...changed. She's turned into one of them."

"What are they?"

"I don't know." Waving his hand at Jas, he added, "This is Jas, she works at the precinct. These creatures are tough and I haven't seen one die yet."

"Why are they killing people? What's wrong with them?"

More questions he couldn't answer, but while Clarissa applied a sticky bandage to his belly, he replied, "I don't know. I don't think anyone knows. The last orders I have are to send people to Kirtland Air Force Base. Effectively the city has fallen and you need to get out."

John nodded at him confidently. "Finally we know where to go. I knew we had to leave, but I didn't know where to take us." Leaning closer to him, he asked, "If we take two cars we can all fit, but what are the roads like out there."

He didn't know John well and looked at him quizzically. "Are you prepared to take everyone out?"

"Hell, yeah. I'm not gonna sit around waiting for some unstoppable asshole to come in here and kill us. The city isn't safe."

Staring at John's creased face and grey hair, he said, "Weapons won't help you. Your best chance is to move fast, and get away from buildings and congested areas. I'd come with you, but my last orders were to tell people to head to the base." Turning to Jas, he added, "You should go with them."

"Nope," she replied dourly. "I'm not doing that. I might not have my badge yet, but your orders are my orders too."

It was obvious she wasn't going to change her mind readily, and he didn't see much point to arguing. "Fine. We'll go with them as far as the outskirts and try to find more survivors as we go. Once they're clear of the city, we'll need to look for more people and help them get to the base."

Turning back to John, he asked, "What kind of car do you have? My Malibu is parked just outside the front door. The biggest risk is getting everyone into the vehicles. Once we're able to move, we'll run down anyone who tries to kill us."

"We should take any food supplies and weapons we have," John replied. "My car is parked on the road and it'll carry five people."

"The roads are pretty congested. You might get stuck," he replied.

"We can't plan for the finer points, Jonesy. We'll just do what we can as we can."

He nodded. "Okay. You can't stay here anyway. I'm not sure what help is coming or even if it is. Your best bet is to get to the base. Hopefully they've got some sort of defense there."

"You mean you don't know?" Louise asked in disbelief.

"No one knows anything right now," he replied. "It's all happened so fast and everyone was affected. It's meant we don't know what troops are left."

"There's no National Guard? No police?" Louise asked in horror.

He shook his head. "I don't know what's left, but whatever there is, it isn't organizing itself quickly."

"That's true, Louise. We haven't seen anything on the street other than the killers and their victims," John added.

"I know, but I assumed there was something somewhere...I mean, who's going to protect us from these murderers?"

"We'll take care of ourselves," John replied firmly.

He'd just lost the woman he'd been with for thirty years, and feeling numb, he nodded to John and said flatly, "That's where it's at."

CHAPTER TWELVE:
A little respect
(Jo)

"It's only been twenty-four hours since the first murders. How can we be losing the cities already?"

She ran her hand through her short, dark hair, and although she'd only washed it the day before, it felt greasy and heavy. Leaning closer to the speaker on her phone, she replied, "It's what happens when one half of the population turns against the other and kills them. It's not something the police force are designed to deal with."

Another impatient voice echoed hollowly through the crackling speaker. "Where are your officers right now? Do you even know?"

Despite her deep exhaustion, she felt a spark of angry indignation at his implied accusation. "Do you have any idea what's happened out here? Or did you just cover your own asses, scuttle into your bunkers, and leave the rest of us to deal with it?"

The original speaker interrupted her. "Okay, there's no need to lose our cool here..."

Glancing out of her window at the smoke from numerous fires oozing across the skyline, she then looked at the street and the clusters of abandoned vehicles. The cars and road were streaked with bloodstains, and the idle bodies of the dead were lying haphazardly in and around the vehicles. After she'd spoken to Jonesy, she'd ordered everyone to evacuate the city and sent the people to the airbase. Unable to get through to anyone in command, she'd made an executive decision, and now they were telling her she'd done the wrong thing.

Clenching her teeth tightly, she replied, "I haven't slept in over thirty-six hours. I'm tired, I'm hungry, I'm alone, and I'm stuck topside in a city full of homicidal maniacs. Don't you dare fucking tell me to stay calm, or I swear I will reach down this line and tear you a new asshole."

"Okay, Commander, we're all under pressure here so let's keep this civil," a voice said sternly.

The past twenty-four hours had frayed her nerves to breaking point and she shouted, "Just shut the fuck up. You have no idea what's going on up here." She knew she was in shock and reacting inappropriately for her rank, but she couldn't stop herself. "You left us!" She roared indignantly. "You abandoned us!" Leaping to her feet, her entire body ached with unused adrenalin. "Outside my window are hundreds of dead bodies. The city is burning. One of my officers saw the murderers leaving the city. They tore their own faces off! They're not human!"

"What...?"

Almost triumphantly, she declared, "Yeah, I thought that might shut you up. Thousands of so-called people were seen leaving the city. I don't know where they were going, but many of them don't look human anymore. It's like...they're shedding their skin and underneath they're a blackened, rubbery sort of creature."

"You mean they were human?"

"I assume so, but I don't know any more than what I've just told you. The city was invaded, which is why I told everyone to head to the base. We need to mount a defense from there." There was no reply from the people on the other end of the line and she asked, "Why don't you know any of this?"

"The President called a state of emergency so we all went to the bunkers, but they had problems. The comms didn't work straight away, and the techs had trouble getting us in contact with one another."

"Are they working now?"

There was a pause and then a voice said, "Yes and no. Some of the bunkers are in contact with one another, but...some aren't responding anymore."

After the insanity of the past day it made perfect sense to her, but it shouldn't have. The invaders were just average people who'd turned into something else, but no one knew who would change and who wouldn't. It was inevitable some of the people who'd gone to the bunkers would turn into killers, and then all hell would have broken loose. Wearily closing her eyes, she imagined what must have happened to the people trapped underground with homicidal maniacs.

With that thought, her eyes popped open again. "Oh, and that's the other problem. The little fuckers bounce. From what I've heard they're almost impossible to kill." Rubbing her eyes tiredly, she asked, "How do you know you're safe where you are? It's very likely some of you will change, and then you've got a real problem to deal with. You can't hide underground. You don't know if the person next to you won't try and kill you."

Her words were met with what seemed to be a stunned silence. A phone in the main office began to ring, but there was no one left to answer it. She didn't want to ignore the phone, it might be one of her officers calling in with an update.

"Just hang on. There's another line ringing."

"Are you the only person there?"

"Yes. I told you. I sent everyone to the airbase."

Not waiting to hear their reply, she walked out of the office and into the main room, trying to work out which phone was ringing. The main room looked as abandoned as it was. Paper was strewn across the floor, and filthy coffee cups were sitting on every desk. She'd long since abandoned her shoes, and padded in her laddered tights to each desk, closing in on the sound of the ringing. Finally, she found the phone in the middle of the cluttered desks.

Picking up the phone from its cradle, she said tersely, "What?"

An almost silent voice whispered, "Help."

"Who are you?"

"Dayton, Doctor Dayton. I'm an Oncologist at the University of New Mexico Hospital on Lomas Boulevard. I'm here with patients and we need help."

She knew the hospital well and had tried to contact it many times, but no one had answered her calls. "What's happening there? I've been trying to get through."

Dayton whispered, "The hospital has been overrun by killers. We managed to escape, but on our way out we found six children under the age of ten in one of the wards. We're hiding in the drug dispensary on the ground floor."

It was clear his situation was desperate, but there was little she could offer to do for him. "Where are the killers now?"

"A lot of them seem to have left, but there's still movement in the corridor. There's only two of us, and we can't easily move six sick children. Some of them are too sick to walk. We need help."

Before she'd sent everyone to the airbase, no one had been responding to their radios for at least two hours, and she didn't expect anyone would now. If there were any police left on the streets, they weren't operating under her command anymore. She didn't have anyone she could send to help them, and she wondered whether the government workers in the bunker could do something.

"Hang on. I'm on another line talking to emergency command, and I'll see what they can do. Stay on the line."

"I'll try, but I'm at the front of the pharmacy counter in the dispensary. If they see me then we're all dead."

Hearing the desperation in Dayton's voice, she replied with a false confidence, "Just hang on. I won't be more than a few minutes."

Carefully placing the phone on the table, she sprinted in her stockinged feet to the conference room with the speakerphone. Leaning over the table, she said rapidly, "I'm on the phone to a Doctor Dayton at University Hospital. There are two adults and six sick children hiding in the drug dispensary on the ground level. Can you send a squad to get them out?"

When no one answered her, she demanded impatiently, "Well?"

"Umm...we don't have a squad to send. That's why we've been trying to get in contact with the police precincts. We're trying to establish what forces there are on the ground."

"But what about the National Guard...and the Army?"

"Before we were told to report to the bunkers, all military personnel were ordered to report in. They recalled all troops overseas, and last we heard they're on their way home."

"Where are they now?"

Again there was silence and then another voice said, "We don't know. No one is exempt from this disease and getting through to anyone anywhere is patchy. Even if anyone answers our calls, they don't necessarily have a situation report for us. The last time we got through to Kirtland Air Force Base, a cleaner answered the call and he didn't know anything other than the base was in chaos."

The direness of their situation was finally becoming real to her. She'd ordered everyone to the base under the assumption the National Guard or Army would roll into the city and get the situation under control. If the secured command units couldn't talk to anyone above ground who could do anything, then it meant no one was coming. She was alone in a city full of corpses and killers.

Frustration overwhelmed her fatigue and she shouted, "How could you have gotten this so wrong? We've come under attack! We've been invaded! All you're doing is sitting on your fat asses thinking you're safe underground. You're useless!" Her spike of anger was satiated and she added bitterly, "In fact, you're worse than useless. You were supposed to be in control, but you're not, and now we've got no way to protect our citizens."

A new voice, one she hadn't heard before during the call, said calmly, "I'm Colonel Bill Ketcher and I couldn't agree with you more. Tell your doctor to hang on. One way or another I'll get a squad to you."

"Just how are you going to do that from a bunker, Colonel?" She asked skeptically.

When he chuckled, she could sense his warmth through the tinny phone line. "I won't be in the bunker. Excuse my language, ma'am, but there's fuck all I can do from down here. I'll go topside and find you a squad, or I'll go to the hospital myself. One way or another, I'll get them the help we owe them."

Despite only hearing his voice for the first time, she heard the steely determination in his tone. Feeling slightly less agitated, she asked, "What do you want me to do?"

"Well, I'm sure as the Commander that you can handle a gun. For the time being, can you stay at your post? You can be my contact into the city. Once I locate the troops, I'll make sure we get you out."

She hadn't thought about leaving yet, and wasn't sure she could even if she wanted to. "I can stay here and man the phones for anyone who is still trying to talk to us, but the doctor and those kids should take priority."

"I agree, but I won't forget you. I'll try and call whenever I can to keep you up-to-date on progress. I'll also need a sitrep from you."

Not only was his voice steady, so was his thinking. It was clear he was already making a plan and, although she was aware it might not work, at least he was being proactive and prepared to risk his own life. "Okay, but, Colonel..."

"I think we can dispense with formalities. Just call me Bill."

Sitting alone at the large conference table, she nodded as if the man was sitting with her. "Okay, Bill, I don't want to tell you how to do your job, but I recommend you bring as much firepower as you can. These...creatures aren't easy to kill and they want you dead. If they see you then they will try to kill you. There's no negotiation."

Bill gave such a deep sigh she heard it clearly through the crackling phone line. "That's the way of any enemy, ma'am, they always want us dead, and it's our job to beat them to the punch."

Despite her circumstance, she found herself smiling at his practical take on their situation. "If we're dispensing with formalities, then you can call me Jo."

A part of her wanted to keep listening to Bill's steady voice and attitude, but she worried she might lose the phone connection to Dayton. "I don't want to stop talking to you, Bill, but I need to talk to the doctor. He's waiting for me to tell him what we're gonna do."

"Go do that. By the time you get back I'll be getting ready to head out, but I will call you, Jo, I promise. Stay near this phone and wait for my call."

She was already half out of her chair, but she leaned closer to the speaker. "You can count on it. Travel safe, Bill."

Without waiting to hear his reply, she turned and ran into the main room towards the phone that was still lying on the desk.

"Dayton?"

"Yes."

"They're sending troops to get you. Stay low and wait."

CHAPTER THIRTEEN:
Hard landing
(Leon)

The plane was skidding to a bumpy halt, and a tangle of bodies was falling from the open door. Lexie had managed to yank him onto the platform, and was holding his arm with one heavily gloved hand. Bodies were still sliding past him and falling onto the tarmac, where some remained motionless, but others were immediately springing to their feet and running towards the cluster of small buildings. Once the plane finally stopped, Lexie pulled him with her as she jumped from the platform. With her fast pace, he felt himself literally flying across the tarmac.

She flicked the lower half of her helmet up and shouted, "They're gonna blow it. I can see the missile."

As they threw themselves to the ground, the plane exploded into pieces, and he prayed none would hit him. Loud gunfire could be heard all around them, and he tried to bury himself deeper into the grass. He had no idea where Tuck and Billy were, but he wasn't optimistic knowing they could have turned, fallen from the plane, or been killed by the explosion. Lifting his head from the dusty ground, he tried to see what was going on. A number of heavily armored vehicles were driving across the airstrip, and shooting at the men and women running towards the buildings.

Lexie was cautiously climbing to her feet, and then she leaned down and easily pulled him from the ground. "Come on. You need to get onto one of the trucks."

Judging by the sound, they were firing .50-cal weapons that seemed to be having some effect, but not as much as he would have expected. Some of the running forms were falling to the ground under the barrage of gunfire, and then climbing to their feet again. Lexie was pulling him towards one of the moving vehicles, and when she caught up with it she waved at the gunner. The truck came to a stop and hands reached out to pull him on board. She didn't join him, but turned and ran towards the running soldiers.

"Don't shoot her with the fifty cal. You'll kill her."

"Roger that," a voice replied.

Now inside the truck, he turned to the man next to him. "What the hell is going on?"

"We're under attack."

"By what?"

"Our own people."

"I know that. I was on the plane, but what the hell is going on?"

"The cities are falling. People just went crazy and started killing one another."

It didn't make any sense to him. "But how did we lose the cities?"

"Sheer volume of the assault. It looks like at least half the population went completely fucking nuts. We've had people turn here too, but a fifty cal to the chest or head puts them down." The plain faced soldier leaned in and said grimly, "But if you want 'em to stay down, you'd best blow their heads off."

Giving him a look of disbelief, he asked, "What the hell survives a fifty cal round to the chest?"

"I dunno, but they're not...human. They're built like black rubber. There doesn't seem to be anything in them...you know, like organs. They're fuckin' hard to kill."

That explained a lot about what had just gone wrong on the plane. Nothing had seemed to stop the killers. An attack on their homeland was a serious change of circumstances, and he hoped they had it under control. "What are our orders?"

"We're being sent to the cities all over the country to try and take them back."

"You mean we've lost them?"

"Like I said, the cities have fallen. Everyone is being deployed to the cities, but command is kinda patchy. We keep losing officers."

"What do you mean?"

The soldier gave him a worried look. "They keeping turning into freaks."

"Woah, check out that ninja!" Another voice exclaimed.

Peering through the narrow slit in the truck, he watched Lexie hammer a running man to the ground. Not content to just bring him down, she slammed her foot against his head repeatedly. Whatever she was doing worked and the man didn't move again.

"We need more of that kinda action."

"Well, there isn't anymore, she's a prototype," he replied.

"She? Isn't it a robot?"

"Don't be dumb, of course not. It's a woman and it's a new tech they've been testing. It's crap," he replied dourly.

"Doesn't look like crap to me."

"Well, it is. She's blind and the whole set up drains power." Pausing, he added, "She can't survive a fifty cal, and when she runs out of power she can't move."

Nodding brusquely, the soldier said, "Prototype or not, we're gonna need more of that tech."

He supposed they would and wondered how advanced they were in their production runs. He remembered Lexie had noticed a man with an odd read on the flight, and thought that maybe her visor was able to detect the people who would go nuts. If that was the case, then they would need more visors as well as the armor and hydraulics.

Between Lexie and the armored trucks with .50-cal weapons, they'd managed to bring down most of the turned soldiers. Some had escaped, but none had made it into the buildings on the air base. Being a small airbase, there was nowhere for them to convene, and he found himself being sent to another plane. After his last experience he didn't really want to board it, but he was being sent to Albuquerque. He had just climbed through the main doors to the C-17, when he heard Tuck calling his name.

Staring down the rows of seats, he saw Tuck's dark hair and waved. "You made it!" When he finally shuffled down the aisle, he threw himself into the chair next to Tuck. "Have you seen Billy?"

Tuck shook his head, "No, I don't think he made it."

"Have you seen Lexie?"

"Nope."

The plane was only half-full, and just before they pulled the doors closed, Lexie pushed her way on board. With her helmet off, she wore her thick, dark visor, and her short blonde hair was a tangled, sweaty mess. Pushing past the men at the door, she made her way towards them carrying several large rugged black boxes with handles.

Puffing, she dropped the boxes in the aisle. "Move over. I need to sit down. This armor is heavy and I'm on half power to conserve my packs."

He flipped up the armrest so she would fit and moved several seats over. "Where's Donna?"

"She's sitting at the back of the plane."

"What's in the boxes?"

"Power chargers, spare visors, repair kits...stuff I need for the gear."

"Why are you coming to Albuquerque?"

"I need to get to CaliTech in California where the techs are." Waving her gloved hand vaguely at her face, she added, "This stuff doesn't maintain itself."

He had a lot of questions to ask her, and he settled back as the plane began gaining speed to take off. "Can you see the people who've turned? Is that what you saw on the other plane?"

Donna had joined them, and she sat on the other side of Lexie listening to their conversation. He couldn't see Lexie's eyes under the thick, dark visor, but she sounded almost bored when she replied, "Everything on the planet emits a different signal. The techs have managed to isolate hundreds of different signals, and the scanners inside the visor reads them. The onboard computer interprets the signals for me. I can't see exactly, but I have a grid with outlines and blobs that represent objects and people to me."

"You haven't answered my question."

Sighing, she replied, "Some people are emitting a signal that's showing as a...green sort of blob. People shouldn't look like that through my visor. Right now I can see you as a pale, pinkish sort of shape." Touching his arm, she added, "And if I touch you I can read your physical status. Your heart rate, blood pressure, temperature and oxygen levels. When I touch the green blobs, I don't get a read. It's like they're dead, only they're still moving."

Giving her a worried look, he asked, "Are there any green blobs on this plane?"

Lexie shook her head. "No, but there weren't on the last plane when we left either."

"When did they show up?"

"I don't know. I had my visor on limited scan to conserve power."

While they'd been talking, Donna had opened one of the rugged boxes and was clearly checking the contents. Leaning across Lexie's armored legs, he asked, "Donna, what's in California?"

"The main design and development labs for this gear."

"Do you work with Lexie?"

"I'm what they call a 'handler'. It's my job to keep her and her gear working. Her shadow nav, Ark, is back at CaliTech in the underground command center. He helps to interpret what she's seeing through her visor and directs her during combat."

He was beginning to understand a Navigator wasn't simply a heavily armored individual with advanced vision, and they relied on a team to keep them operational and effective. "How many Navigators are there?"

"It depends on what you call a Navigator. There are shadow navs that are based in the main lab. They use the satellites to take a direct feed from the visors. Then there are navs only capable of using the visors and not the armor. There's also several types of armor in prototype.

Lexie is in light armor with mid-range hydraulics. We have heavier armor and hydraulics with different weapons systems, but they don't move too fast."

Lexie snorted. "She's talking about the 'tanks'. They're basically heavy duty armor and hydraulics with massive firepower, but they move so slowly I call them turtles."

By now a small group of men and women had formed around their seats, and they were trying to listen to their conversation. One man was leaning over the back of the chair in front of him and he said, "We're gonna need massive firepower. Our standard weapons have no effect on whatever these things are. Even a fifty cal struggles to get them down."

Tapping Donna on the arm to get her attention again, he asked, "How much kit is in California?"

She shrugged. "I don't know. I do know they were training people and shipping raw materials to ramp production, but it got put on hold when the army threatened to cancel the contract."

"How hard is it to learn how to use the gear?" The other man asked.

"It depends on what kind of nav you wanna be. Fully functioning like Lexie takes at least six months, but you can learn to use a visor in a matter of a month, and the tanks just need to be fit."

With a sharp exclamation of disgust, Lexie said bluntly, "As long as you're okay with having your eyeballs replaced." When no one spoke, she added, "That's why I have to get back to CaliTech. I need to be near the techs. What Donna isn't telling you is that the gear is buggy as hell. The software and firmware have conflicts and they're still working on it. My software will already be out-of-date, and I'll need to get the latest version when I get back to the labs."

He looked up at the man leaning over the seat. "I think we need to talk to command about this."

The man nodded at him. "Yeah, we need to get control of those labs."

CHAPTER FOURTEEN:
Waking nightmare
(Ally)

It had taken her a whole year to save enough money for her trip to Johnsondale. Sequoia National Park was somewhere she'd always wanted to go, and she planned to hike the area by taking what she needed with her, then pitching her tent at the many different campgrounds. For most people it wasn't an expensive holiday, but with her short fuse she was prone to losing her job, and was always short on cash. Being fired didn't bother her, she was only earning minimum wage as a waitress, and she didn't care who she served or where she did it. At the age of twenty-six, her life was stalled, but even she had to admit it was largely her own fault. After leaving school, instead of going to college like many others had, she'd taken the less reliable path of modelling and failed dismally at it. It was one thing to be called the prettiest girl in her school, and quite another to convince people to pay her for it.

Although she was raised in Houston, she now shared an apartment in Lynwood, Los Angeles with three other people. Not wanting to go home and admit her life was a total failure, she drove a beat up Toyota, and barely made her rent each month. Even though she wasn't considered pretty enough to make it in the bright lights of LA, she was still a striking looking woman, with long legs and curves in all the right places. Her dark hair, sculpted face and full mouth attracted attention wherever she went, and she was never short of men in her life. More than failing as a model, it was the men in her life that had disappointed her most. They'd lied to her, cheated on her and let her down in more ways than she could count. Her mother had always taught her to smile through her pain, but her face literally ached from trying to pretend none of it hurt when it did. Deciding there were no decent men to be found, she'd dumped the last one less than a week ago, and was determined to stay single.

Now her hard won holiday was ruined as well. While hiking along one of the many trails, she'd slipped awkwardly and twisted her ankle. It wasn't so bad she couldn't walk, but there was no way she could hike the route she'd planned. With her cap pulled low over her eyes, and her heavy backpack pulling against her shoulders, she'd gritted her teeth and limped back to the parking lot. She never seemed to cut a break, and frustration was bubbling up inside her in a way she was finding difficult to repress. Dropping her backpack onto the back seat of her car, she climbed behind the wheel and stared sullenly at the beautiful trees around her. Sighing to herself, she started the car and made her way along the road leading out of the park.

She was sick of being with other people and had wanted five days to herself. By finding secluded areas to set up her one-person tent, she hadn't spoken to anyone in three days. Although she could call her roommates to tell them she was coming home early, her mobile phone had run out of both credits and power. It wasn't as if she was close to them, and she doubted they would care or even notice whether she was home or not. After driving for an hour, her ankle was aching, and the stretch of road in front of her was long and flat. In the distance, she could see a man standing by the side of the road next to his car.

She didn't intend to stop, but as she drew closer, he ran down the middle of the road waving his arms wildly. With her foot still hovering over the accelerator, she slowly came to stop, and wound down her window by no more than a few inches.

"What do you want?" She asked sharply.

The man was wearing filthy jeans with a matching flannel shirt, and he looked sweaty and disheveled. She guessed he was probably in his thirties, and he had an air of panic about him. "Where the hell have you been?"

"What do you mean?"

"Haven't you heard what's happened?"

She wasn't in the mood to play twenty questions, and eyeing the man suspiciously, she pressed the button to wind up her window. Before she could finish, she heard a sharp tapping against the glass, and looked across at the man again. The tapping was being made by a decent sized handgun, which suddenly smashed its way through her window, spraying shattered glass into her lap.

"Unlock the back door!" He shouted.

"What the fuck are you doing?"

He jabbed the gun in her face and snarled, "Open the back door or I'll kill you. One way or another I'm taking this car."

She couldn't believe she was being carjacked. Rather than feeling subdued, her frustration hiked up yet another notch. Outrage filled her and she swore at him. "Fuck you."

"Seriously, babes, I'm not kidding."

The road was empty of any other cars, and it was more than feasible for the man to shoot her. He could easily throw her body out of the car, and there'd be no one to witness her untimely death. It'd be just her luck to die by the side of a dirty road, and end up as a Jane Doe on a slab in a morgue. She reluctantly used the central locking button on her car to release the doors.

Once the man had hurled himself into the seat behind her, she said flatly, "My name's Ally."

She didn't know why she bothered to tell him her name, other than she'd always been told a person had to make themselves human to an attacker, but she doubted it would make any difference with this guy.

"My name's Nigel."

Inwardly she groaned. She was being threatened by some jackass called Nigel, and she could almost read the headlines. 'Woman killed by Nigel', didn't have good ring to it. Life was determined to make a mockery of her existence to the bitter end. The leading emotion coursing through her was one of outrage and indignation, and she couldn't understand why she wasn't frightened. All she wanted to do was turn around and slap him across the head, but the barrel of his gun was still jabbing her in the back of the neck.

Stuffing down her frustration, she asked blandly, "Where do you want me to take you?"

"Anywhere there aren't any people. Head to the desert, babes."

"What? Arizona? Why do you wanna go there?"

"Where the fuck have you been, babes?" The man asked impatiently, while he began to roughly pull items from her backpack.

"Hiking in Sequoia National Park."

Having found a snack bar and water in her backpack, the man scooted across the back seat, and put his feet up on the seat behind her. While he ripped open the health bar, he chuckled. "Oh, so you really don't know." Using the bedroll from her pack, he tucked it behind his head and leaned back. "You shoulda stayed where you were, babes."

"Why?"

"The world's gone to hell, babes. People just woke up one day and started killing one another." With that comment, the man suddenly looked tired, and he leaned his head against the bedroll.

"Why are you carjacking me?"

"San Bernardino went crazy, babes, I barely managed to get out alive." Waving his gun in her direction, he added, "Good thing I had this with me. I was heading to the desert and my car broke down. It's survival of the fittest now, and I'm fitter than you, babes."

His calling her 'babes' was getting on her nerves, and even though he had a gun, she'd pretty much reached the end of her patience. He was telling her some bullshit story about people murdering one another, and that the only safe place was in the desert. The man was clearly out of his mind, and she wanted to smack him for adding his problems to hers.

"Are you gonna let me go?"

"Nah, babes, you should come with me. You're gonna need someone to cover your pretty ass."

He needed to stop calling her babes, it was driving her nuts, and her frustration was turning into rage. Whereas an hour earlier she would have said she was in a bad mood, now she was ready to kill anyone who crossed her. She'd never had a good handle on her temper, and whenever she felt the sharp spike of anger running through her, she would do things she usually didn't really regret later. Her mind registered a large abandoned looking building on the side of the road looming in the near distance, while she continued to argue with the man.

"I'm not going with you."

The man opened his eyes and leaned forward into the back of the front passenger seat. "Listen, babes, I'm telling the truth. There's no TV, no phones, no radio, no nothin'. People have gone nuts, and the cops can't control it. I thought the army would have shown up, but they haven't. You need to come with me, babes, I'll take care of you."

He sounded genuine, but he'd also just carjacked her. There was no way she was going to let some jackass called Nigel shoot her and leave her as a Jane Doe on the side of the road. More importantly, he kept calling her babes, and she couldn't listen to it one more time. Her spark of anger took control, and she violently twisted the steering wheel, slamming her foot down on the accelerator. The car bucked into action, and gathered speed as she headed towards the thick wall of the abandoned building.

"Do. Not. Call. Me. Babes!"

The man never had a chance to plead his case before her car slammed violently into the wall. He was flung past her, over the passenger seat, and head first through the windshield. Her head slammed forward into the deployed airbag, and she felt the seatbelt cut savagely into her chest plate. In the movies, she would have expected to hear the wailing of sirens as someone came to her rescue, but silence reigned. Every so often she would become aware of her surroundings, the dryness of the air, the heat or the cold. She didn't seem to be able to hold onto her consciousness, and reality would drift away until she surfaced again.

Eventually she became conscious again and was able to stay vaguely aware. The blood on her face had dried, and when she tried to lift her head from the airbag, she felt her skin tear. Her head felt strangely heavy, and she rolled it back onto the headrest, while trying to make sense of her surroundings. The road she'd been driving along was on her left, and the man was crumpled across the hood of her car. He had his back to her, but there was blood across the hood, and it trailed thickly down the side of her car. His blood had already become brown and hardened, and she guessed she'd been unconscious for a long time.

If she didn't get out of the car, she would die. Her body felt stiff and bruised, and she gingerly tried to move her left arm. It was working, but everything felt tight, and pain ripped through her shoulder. Groaning, she fumbled for the door handle, managing to pull it open.

Now the door was unlatched she needed to push it, but lacked the strength in her arm. The magical sirens and helpful people had never materialized, and she didn't understand why no one had stopped to investigate a crashed car by the side of the road. Using her right arm to brace herself against the passenger seat, she pushed her body into the door until it swung open. The movement sent shockwaves of pain down her spine and legs, but at least her ankle didn't hurt anymore.

She needed to get to the road where someone might see her. Allowing herself to fall from the car, she landed with a thump, and it jarred her already bruised body. Standing didn't seem to be an option, and she began to claw her way across the pebbly dirt, hoping to eventually reach the tarmac. Her arms and legs were working for her, but they felt weak and shaky. Her head hurt in a way she'd never felt before, and all her previous worries became insignificant. Feeling the dryness in her mouth, she realized she was badly dehydrated, and if she didn't get water soon, that would be the thing that would kill her. She was only twenty-six years old and didn't want to die, she wasn't done with life yet. Inching her way across the dirt, bits of dust blew into her eyes, making her vision bleary. The hopelessness of her situation threatened to overwhelm her, but she was too dry to cry.

It wasn't fair. She'd barely had a chance to live. Every dream she'd ever had was already crushed, and she was going to be left to die by the side of a road. Nobody cared enough to even know where she was to know she was missing. What had she ever done to deserve to die like this? Her unspoken question made her angry. She was a decent person and she deserved better. How dare the world destroy her life this way. The more she thought about it the harder she clawed at the ground beneath her. She was angrier now in what she guessed were her last moments on earth than she'd ever been. Unable to do anything with her rage, she determinedly dragged at the ground, and was rewarded with the hard texture of tarmac. She'd finally reached the road, and exhausted, she felt her mind drift away again.

CHAPTER FIFTEEN:
Born again
(Steve)

His mind was fragmenting into a million little pieces and he was resisting its collapse. Behind him were hundreds of thousands of people following him across the desert like devoted fans. None of them spoke to him and he didn't try to talk to them either. Anyone who crossed their path that didn't belong with them was immediately slaughtered, but mostly people headed in the opposite direction when they saw them coming.

He stopped and stared at the sandy, scrubby land ahead of him. Immediately the people behind him stopped, and he finally turned to face them. Most of them were missing large patches of their flesh, and beneath their human form was a black, rubbery body. His own body was mostly a blackened surface now, and he thought he looked a bit like a soldier ant. The change didn't bother him, and he was relieved the irritating itchy sensation had finally stopped.

Wanting to get a better view of the people following him, he climbed a low hill while they patiently watched him. It was only then he saw just how many people had followed him out of the city. At least two hundred thousand men, women and children were standing almost in a formation of rows and columns. He didn't understand why they'd followed him or what they wanted. As if his entourage had understood his unspoken question, they began to rearrange themselves into groups. Without pushing, shoving or speaking, they slowly clustered themselves into teams, but he didn't understand their logic.

A group of what he guessed were five thousand or more to his left began to shudder and shake. It was strange to watch, and if he hadn't known better, he would have thought they were having some sort of a fit. A woman at the front of the group hunched her shoulders and began to heave. Slowly a black webbing emerged from her spine, and he realized she was growing wings. They were slightly sheer and black, with a thick, twisted rope running through them. At full width, the wings spread six feet behind her and were attached to the entire length of her arms. Her arms and legs lengthened and became thinner, and her wings began to vibrate. Suddenly her feet lifted from the ground, and her shoes landed on the desert floor, blowing dust into the air. Her movement was copied by all the others in her group, and they began to rise above the rest of the followers.

Another group began to undulate, becoming shorter and squat, until freed from their clothes, they sat like black turtles about three feet high. To his surprise, they began to scuttle about, crashing into one another until they formed a circle, and began to burrow rapidly into the sandy earth. All four of their shortened and thick limbs worked frantically into the dry ground, and they hit a denser layer under the sandy surface. Dirt began to fly into the air as they furiously tore into the earth, and he was stunned at how quickly a deep crater was forming around them. Their feet were shaped like shovels, with a row of thick, six-inch long claws on each end. With their stumpy wide limps, they dug powerfully into the ground, scattering the dirt behind them with an effortless fury.

Before he had time to absorb the impact of the diggers, another group began to evolve. Skinny, insect like legs sprung from their torso, and tipped them over until they were parallel with the land. At least twenty legs, ten on each side, held them about two feet above the earth, and they began to move rapidly around the area in front of him. Seeming to want to prove their worth, they sprinted around wildly, until one finally paused in front of him. What was once a human head had changed until it was a smooth black dome, and he couldn't work out where its eyes were. The arms and legs had been absorbed into its body, and only the twenty insect-like limbs remained. These creatures resembled fat, squat spiders, and they leapt over and on top of one another with manic speed. Their sharp, jerky movement made it difficult to guess which direction they would go. Clustered together as they were, the motion became a blur of angry buzzing, and the air filled with the loud rustling of thousands of bodies endlessly colliding with one another.

Clearly not wanting to be outdone, another group began to shake uncontrollably and grew taller. Their arms, legs and torsos became bulkier, and their heads expanded until they were smooth and bullet-shaped. In the middle of their featureless faces was a spout with a hole in the end. Their human skin split and fell away from their bodies, until they stood nine feet tall, with broad shoulders and heavy torsos. As they began to stomp heavily towards him, he noticed unlike their brother species, they lumbered with a steady gait. Struggling to understand the point of their type, he was quickly educated when one spat a long stream of fluid into the air from the spout in the middle of its oval head. It arced twenty feet and landed on the sand, which began to bubble and burn with its touch.

All of the groups erupted into a frenzy of motion as they evolved into the species they really were. More flyers rose high into the sky, and the spitters grew tall around the squat diggers. Two hundred thousand creatures, that moments before still resembled their human ancestry, expanded or shrank, abandoning clumps and sheets of human flesh as they did. His army was forming before his eyes and it felt familiar and right. Glancing at his own body, he shrugged off the last of his clothes and skin from his rubbery, black and angular frame. Like him, all the other creatures were composed of the same substance, and he knew they belonged to him.

The changes in his body and those around him stripped his brain of the last of its humanity, and he explored his new way of being. As a human he'd lived inside his own mind, and he could only see, hear, sense and touch what was in front of him. His new mind didn't work the same way. All the creatures in front of him were extensions of himself. They weren't separate beings, but a part of him that responded to his instructions just as the arms and legs attached to his body did. It was a strange way to live. His existence was spread across not just the two hundred thousand bodies he could see, but many more that were located in other places. He didn't just control them, they were him.

The barriers of his being collapsed, and suddenly he could see through thousands of eyes, order their limbs, and make them move and do what he wanted. He was a creature with potentially millions of parts, and his mind was able to direct them all as unconsciously as he controlled his own body.

"I am the brain that rules the parts."

He thought he'd spoken, but it didn't sound like the words he'd once used. Instead, a high-pitched squeal emerged from not just him, but all the other bodies he owned. The noise exploded into the silent desert like a high-pitched wail cutting through static.

With his mind in a million parts, he could see cities burning and humans dying. He was taking control of the planet, and his millions of bodies were doing exactly what he wanted. They were tearing the world apart just as he expected them to.

"We are dominant."

Again his voice was echoed as a high-pitched wail by the thousands of bodies around him. He was the brain and he would dominate the land. It was his sole purpose for existence, and the wailing creatures around him formed part of his body. Under his direction, they would kill anything that threatened him. As the brain he needed to be kept safe, and the diggers began to frantically rip deeper into the earth. Large mounds of sand were forming around the hole they were creating. The spitters were dampening the dry earth, and it began to form into hard lumps. He needed a nest, somewhere he would be safe from any species that threatened his domination.

While his many arms and legs did what he wanted, the last remnants of his human mind collapsed.

CHAPTER SIXTEEN:
Eyes without a face
(Ark)

"Where the hell are they going?"

"What do you mean?"

"They're walking into the desert. Why would they be doing that? What's out there?"

He was sitting in the underground command center near Johnsondale in the Sequoia National Forest, observing their movement through one of the satellites. Lexie had powered down and he couldn't see through her anymore. She'd told him she was running short of power packs, and would use local viewing only, which meant he couldn't access her visor. With nothing much to do, he'd taken to monitoring the images from the satellites sweeping across the land and cities, trying to understand what was happening.

He'd joined CaliTech a year earlier to provide design advice for the militarization of their technology. Having lost his legs in a combat incident the year before he'd joined them, he was grateful to find a job that used his skills and allowed him to continue his ongoing rehabilitation. The Army paid for his medical expenses, but the top up of private health cover allowed him to receive additional treatments, without waiting in what seemed like an endless queue of wounded troops. With the severity of his injuries, almost the only parts of him he could use to work were his brains and his eyes, and with his military training, he made an excellent shadow navigator.

The visor technology had fascinated him and it still did. It was able to detect anything within the electromagnetic spectrum, including infrared, gamma rays, microwaves, ultraviolet, radio and magnetic signals. The sensors could detect movement, see through walls, and using RF imaging they could analyze fluids. It was impressive tech, all shrunk to fit inside a visor and capture data that could be interpreted by the Navigator, and then relayed via satellites to the shadow navs. From what he'd understood, the hydraulics and armor had only been added so the visor could be used in combat. CaliTech wanted to become the one stop shop to supply personal kit for every boot on the ground. Given there were hundreds of thousands of combat troops in the U.S. alone, it would add up to a substantial contract that would run for decades.

When it came to using the visor, Lexie was their most capable Navigator, and he'd actively pursued her to become her shadow nav. Following her every move, he was able to direct her through a series of combat trials to fully test the functionality of the tech. Given she had no military training, he'd struggled to keep her moving through the ever changing pace of a simulated war zone. She often hesitated or panicked, and would stop in the middle of a simulation. He'd learned there was one other part of him that CaliTech needed, and that was his ability to yell. Sitting in their underground bunker, surrounded by large screens, controls, keyboards and microphones, he was often heard swearing like the trooper he really was. With practice, he'd learned when to soothe and when to shout at Lexie, and used both tactics liberally.

For all his frustration with her, he missed her when she wasn't online. The Navigators referred to it as being 'on the grid'. The grid was actually a shared comms platform where they could all talk to one another informally. Through the right devices and with security clearance, anyone could add themselves to the grid and join the conversation. Today the grid was filled with more questions than answers as people tried to understand what was going on. The phones lines, both land and mobile, were grinding to a halt, and the television network had been off the air for over a day.

Attached to the comms room was another area with a bathroom, several bunks, and a small kitchenette. He and the other two shadow navs lived underground for up to a month at a time, until they were rotated onto a week's leave. The last instructions they'd received were to stay where they were, and that the building was in lockdown. The lunatic Chief Executive was paranoid, and he'd designed the enormous four-story building to shutter down in the case of an emergency. That meant the windows were now blocked and the heavy security gates would be closed.

CaliTech was hidden deep inside the national park and surrounded by several tall walls. It was two miles in diameter and inside the heavily protected perimeter were a collection of buildings. The main building housed the production site, Executive offices, and Command Center where he was sitting. The Research and Development labs were in a large building next to it with a small hospital facility. On the other side of the main building was an enormous hangar used to train the Navigators. Directly opposite the main building were the living quarters for the shift workers and it also contained the cafeteria and gymnasium. The site also had several decent sized warehouses filled with various supplies and gear.

The grounds around the cluster of buildings were used to simulate battle conditions, and there were various locations the Navigators used for combat testing. To help trial the technology, there were a range of typical combat vehicles and several helicopters on the grounds. They even had an armory with a wide range of weapons and artillery to test how well the tech stood up under real battle conditions. When he'd first arrived, he was surprised they were allowed to have so much weaponry outside of a military base, but it seemed that CaliTech had friends in very high places in Washington.

All of the technology was built by hand in an enormous production site on the ground floor of the main building. No one would ever tell him just how much kit the Chief Executive had built in anticipation of the multi-billion-dollar order from the US military, but he suspected the man had a lot of it stored in the warehouses. Rumor had it he'd undertaken a form of up-market crowdfunding, and raised billions from wealthy patrons all over the world. A lot of the money was supposedly from the Middle East, and he wondered if they knew they were funding the future army that could ultimately defeat them. He didn't have much faith in the technology as it was currently being proposed. The idea of blinding soldiers, and making them so dependent on a power source and satellites struck him as naïve at best, and was more likely outright stupid.

"Why are there so many people in the one place?"

That was the question he'd just asked, and he replied dourly, "I dunno. I just asked you that question."

The man sitting at the half circle next to him surrounded by his own screens was called Dom, but privately he'd nicknamed him Dim. The guy seemed to suffer from Asperger's Syndrome, and although he was an outstanding shadow nav, he was pretty stupid in every other way.

"Why do they read so weird?"

He didn't have an answer to that question either. When he switched to infrared they weren't showing on his screen at all, which implied they weren't radiating any heat. It had to be a fault with their software and it wasn't interpreting their bodies correctly. They'd tracked the large group of people from Albuquerque to where they'd all stopped in the middle of the desert near Pueblo Pintado. He desperately wanted to zoom in and get a closer image of what was going on, but they didn't have enough control over the satellites to do that. They didn't usually use the satellites for their visuals, instead they relied on the data from their Navigator's visor, and all he could see through the satellite image was a grainy picture of a large number of people in the desert.

Amber rolled her chair across the small room until she was positioned behind him. Leaning on his shoulder, she asked, "So, what do we do now? We've been stuck down here for over twenty-four hours, and no one's telling us anything. Maybe we should head upstairs and find out what's going on."

"I think we know as much as anyone does right now. The cities have come under attack and the troops have been recalled to sort it out."

"I'm worried about Frank and the kids. I thought the lockdown would be finished by now."

Amber was married and had a couple of young children. CaliTech paid them all incredibly well, and she was now the primary income earner for her family. She was able to work their odd schedule by leaving her husband to take care of their home and the children. The shadow navs had to be online anytime the Navigators were. With ten Navigators of various types testing the gear, their small team worked around the clock to support them. They only had three shadow navs, and they worked in shifts to provide twenty-four-hour support, but it didn't really work that way. The shadow navs were like an extension of the field-based Navigator, and they either bonded with them or they didn't. He worked almost exclusively with Lexie, and the other shadow navs each had their favorites.

"You can't go out there on your own. There's something going very wrong," he replied with genuine concern. "Maybe we can get one of the navs to escort you home."

"Who's up there?" She asked, referring to the Navigators that were inside the main building.

"I think Tank is around."

Tank wasn't the guy's real name, but no one ever called him by any other. The 'tanks', as they were nicknamed, were their latest attempt to satisfy the Army's concern about blinding their soldiers to use the visors. It was reasonable concern, but not replacing their eyes with orbs meant they had a lot less advanced vision through their visors. The techs had focused on improving the armor to such an extent it was less vulnerable to even a .50-cal weapon. In addition to the thickened armor, the tanks also carried heavy-duty guns that wrapped across their shoulders and fitted to their arms. They fired .50-cal bullets, and could launch grenades from their shoulder packs. The rest of their armor housed large power packs to compensate for the demands of their heavier gear and stronger hydraulics. The tanks weren't nimble and they lumbered with a steady gait. The intention was to use the lighter Navigators with advanced vision to recon the enemy, and the tanks were designed to hammer their way through enemy lines.

"Do you think they'll fire me if I leave?"

He understood her concern. CaliTech were a humorless group of Executives hell-bent on building the most powerful defense company on earth, and meeting with the faceless suits was always a trial. Instead of asking for a meeting, they would tell them they needed to 'reach out' to them. If anyone dared to suggest their family needed them, it was met with a puzzled expression as if 'family' was a foreign word. They bandied around terms like 'innovation' and told people to 'find creative solutions', but any suggestions that didn't align to their rigid objectives were politely listened to and then ignored. CaliTech was fond of referring to themselves as 'the family', when in reality they were a dictatorial, unyielding and inhumane machine dedicated to achieving their endgame.

Swiveling his electric chair and dislodging her from his shoulder, he eyed her decisively. "Just go. If they ask why you left, I'll tell them I told you to leave. But be careful, there's something going very wrong here, and I don't think it's safe out there."

Amber gave him a grateful look. "I'll see if I can find Tank."

"Stay on the grid and give me some on the ground feedback. And wear one of the Tank visors...and make sure Tank's armed..."

"He's not allowed to leave the grounds armed," Dom declared accusingly.

From everything he'd seen, he suspected absolutely everyone was now armed, and those that weren't were most likely dead. "Dom, you need to keep up. It looks like every city is under attack, and I haven't seen an adequate military response. Commercial planes have been grounded, and there's not enough jets in the air to indicate a controlled or complete defense. It looks like a war zone out there."

"Do you think it's that bad?" Amber asked worriedly.

All their Navigators other than Lexie were either missing or grounded in the main building, but he'd seen enough through the satellites to know the cities were burning. More than a few large groups of people had left the cities, and were heading for open areas in the surrounding country. What worried him most was how quickly some of them seemed to be moving. Normal people only walked at a certain pace and took breaks, but from what he'd seen these groups didn't stop. Every major city had hundreds of thousands of people moving at a steady clip to a clear area outside of the city, and he didn't know why. If he still had his legs, he would gear up and take a look for himself, but he wasn't exactly mobile anymore. When he'd first arrived at CaliTech he'd asked if they could build him a set of hydraulic limbs. They'd told him that would involve designing robotics and that wasn't what they did. Nonetheless, one of the engineers had viewed his request as a challenge, and he was quietly optimistic they might be able to do something for him.

For the moment, he needed to wait for Lexie to land and make her way to their site. Once she returned, they could regroup and send her and the other Navigators to recon the region around them. Using the Navigators as his arms and legs, he could gain the visibility he needed to learn what was really going on.

Turning to face Amber, he replied, "I don't know how bad it is, but better to be safe than sorry. I'll talk to Tank and make sure he's ready to roll."

CHAPTER SEVENTEEN:
Lost in the city
(Bill)

It had been a while since he'd done what he thought of as real soldiering. He was what was known as a 'lifer' in the army, and starting as a Second Lieutenant, he'd worked his way up to his current position as a Colonel. Having been deployed to Desert Storm, Somalia, Iraq and Afghanistan, he hadn't covered himself in medals, but he'd been a calm and effective leader. He considered himself a steady and even-tempered man, not prone to emotional outbursts, but approachable enough to win the trust of the men and women who followed him. His current assignment was as the Army liaison for emergency planning, which was how he'd found himself inside the bunker. According to the plan, he was supposed to maintain contact with the troops above ground, and keep the heads of government posts informed about their situation, capabilities and deployments.

The plan had sounded good on paper, but like so many do, this one had proven to be a bust in practice. He hadn't been able to stay in contact with the military contacts above ground. Even when he'd tried the standard lines to the bases, anyone he managed to speak to hadn't had a clue what was going on. From the little he'd been able to gather, the command structure had collapsed when many of their officers had turned into killers. Just as one murderous officer was replaced, the next one would start out sane and then go crazy. Eventually there were so many conflicting orders from different Commanding Officers, no one knew what they were supposed to be doing.

The bunker wasn't doing well either. In theory, all the services to support and defend the city were represented inside the bunker, and they could monitor and direct the work of the teams above ground. He supposed government workers didn't transform into heroes overnight, and they'd approached the problem by running a never-ending series of non-productive meetings. It wasn't like the movies, where everyone was always shown to be competent and completely focused on the immediate crisis. In the real world, people worried about their families, and many were unable to adapt fast enough to the emerging situation. With the continual breakdown in communications, they lacked accurate, comprehensive and up-to-date information. Without information they couldn't make decisions, and without communication, they couldn't tell anyone what to do even if they made any.

Hearing Jo on the conference line had filled him with hope. At least someone was at their post and keeping their shit wired tight. He wasn't sure he agreed with her assessment that they'd been invaded, but sending civilians out of the city and to the air force base was a reasonable way to proceed. Losing the police force, and having no sight of the National Guard and Army, had left her with few options to protect the civilians. She either had to tell them to stay inside with their doors locked, or get the hell out of the city. Neither option was a good one, but given people could turn into killers without warning, staying in their homes wasn't going to save them. At least the base was armed, and they could put up a good fight against anyone who turned into a killer.

He'd already left the bunker and found himself on a road that, according to his map, would lead him across the city and towards the base. If he went left, he could find himself a vehicle and drive to the base. If he went right, it would lead him across the city where he could easily locate the precinct where he'd told Jo to wait. If he went to the base, he might be able to find a squad, and either lead or send them to the hospital. If he went to the precinct, he could find Jo and they could go to the hospital together. He wasn't usually an indecisive man, but he was torn between taking command at the base, and finding Jo and saving the kids at the hospital.

He had no idea what condition the base was in, and could only assume if no military had been deployed then it wasn't good. It was very possible the command structure had collapsed to such an extent there would be no one there he could deploy. In the end, he made a purely emotional decision, and it was Jo who was trapped in the precinct alone, waiting for him to help her leave. The internet wasn't working, so he was relying on his memory of the city maps. He estimated he was about ten miles from the precinct, and decided he could cover the distance easier on foot. Strapped to his back was a pack filled with ammo, batteries, water and food. He hadn't been sure what he'd find topside, but based on Jo's advice, he was carrying an M4A1, two handguns and a KABAR.

The region outside of the bunker was made up of wide roads, light industrial buildings and clusters of private residences. If he travelled the side streets, he expected there were more homes with the usual schools, churches and shops. He wasn't interested in the area, and tried to visualize the fastest route on foot to the precinct. Since he'd emerged from the concealed secondary entrance to the bunker, he hadn't heard much of anything. As he walked right onto the I-40 that should lead him in the direction of the precinct, he was surprised to hear a vehicle heading towards him.

Unsure of the situation, he ducked behind an abandoned vehicle, crouched low and peered over the trunk. The road was straight and six lanes wide, but it was cluttered with abandoned and crashed cars. He didn't really understand where all the people had gone, and assumed they'd either left, or were hiding in the surrounding buildings. There was broken glass all over the road, and the vehicle he was hiding behind had bullet holes punched along the side. Wearing his fatigues and army boots, he was grateful for his knee and shin protectors.

The car he'd heard was travelling slowly down the road, clearly trying to navigate around the vehicles spread across it. When it finally came into view, it turned out to be a GMC Yukon. The driver wasn't visible behind the tinted windshield, and the car had large dents down the side. He tried to decide whether to flag the car down, or to let it pass without revealing himself. In the end, he procrastinated long enough for the car to drive slowly past him, and caught sight of the driver in the side window. The man was huge, with a shaved head and facial tattoos that reached to his collar. There were several more men in the back of the car holding long-nosed guns. Recognizing their type, he believed he could have defended himself, but it wasn't worth the fight.

Once the car had passed, he stood and continued at a steady clip towards the taller buildings at the center of the city. The closer he got the more obvious it became just how far the city had fallen, and he lost count of the number of broken bodies he passed. They'd taken on the ashen color of the dead, many were covered in flies, and some looked as if they'd already been mauled by animals.

Being so close to the center of the city, he assumed there must be packs of dogs already running wild. Shop fronts and the glassed entrances to office buildings were smashed, or filled with holes surrounded by shattered glass. Firefights had clearly taken place, and he wondered where the victors were. Passing by a small deli, he peered into the darkened interior. The shelves were half-empty and crushed products were scattered across the floor. He noticed some food was left on the shelves, but that wasn't a good sign. If people were hiding in the buildings, they should have raided the shop and stripped it bare of any supplies.

The smell of smoke was lingering in the air, and he tried to locate any still burning fires. Nothing was visible, but the buildings around him were taller and the skyline was disappearing. What worried him the most was the silence. The wind was blowing down the narrower roads of the city, and paper and other litter was rustling in the breeze, but there were no sounds of vehicles or people. The city had shut down, and other than him, no one was moving on the streets. The number of pale and dusty looking corpses littering the roads was growing. Some were so badly damaged it was hard to tell whether he was looking at a man or a woman, and it was the bodies of the children that clutched at his gut. The streets were becoming more congested with corpses than cars, and he wondered just how many more bodies he'd find inside the buildings. Jo's anger with the men and women in the bunker made more sense to him now, and he pressed on, anxious to find her.

As he passed what appeared to be an office building, a low whistle caught his attention. Stopping, he trained his weapon at the narrow alleyway between the buildings. The whistle stopped abruptly and he called, "Identify yourself."

"Put your gun down. I'm human."

The man's answer puzzled him, but using the wall for cover, he continued to train his gun in the direction the voice came from. "What does that mean?"

"Are you the army?"

He had no intention of telling the man he was alone and said sternly, "You didn't answer my question."

In the shadow of the alley, a man stood up from inside a large dumpster. His face was so filthy he couldn't tell how old the man was, only that he was tall and leanly built.

"What are you doing in the dumpster?"

The man hadn't moved, but said in a low voice, "Shh, you'll wake them up."

"Wake who up?"

"The aliens."

Recalling Jo's description of the killers, he asked, "You mean the rubbery, black creatures?"

Flicking his hand to indicate he should move closer to him, the man replied impatiently, "Yes, yes, where have you been?"

Walking across to the man, he looked up at him still standing inside the large dumpster. "Why are you in the trash?"

"It's safer here."

"Safer than where?"

"Than being on the street or in the buildings."

"Why aren't the buildings safe?"

The man's face was creased with grime, and his filthy eyebrows shot up in surprise. "Because that's where they came from. They're still in there killing anyone they can find. You can't stay in the buildings. It isn't safe."

"But you can't be on the streets either?"

Grinning with satisfaction, the man replied, "That's why I'm in the trash."

The guy was clearly off his meds and he shook his head. "You need to get out of the city and head for Kirtland Air Force Base."

"No way. I'd never make it out alive. I know where to hide on the streets. I ain't leaving."

Comprehension was slowly dawning on him and he asked, "Is this where you live? On the streets?"

The man nodded enthusiastically. "Yeah, I lost my apartment when I lost my job. I lived in my car for a while, but it broke. Now I live on the streets."

"Did you see what happened?"

He nodded again. "Oh, yes. People were shooting at one another, but it didn't do them any good. You can't shoot an alien. They just kept attacking until the people died."

"Why do you think they're aliens?"

Giving him a look of disbelief, he replied, "Because they look like aliens."

"What do they look like?"

"Black with smooth faces and no eyes. Hands like thin claws." The man held up his own filth encrusted hands as if they were talons.

"Do they talk?"

"No, no, no. They screech like a hawk with prey, only they don't eat their victims, they just kill them." Almost as an afterthought, he added, "It makes you wonder why they kill them."

"Where are they now?"

The man shrugged dismissively. "Some left. Some are still here." Narrowing his eyes, he said knowingly, "Nowhere is safe."

The man had witnessed the fall of the city and survived, and despite his apparent insanity, there was a reasonable chance he knew what he was talking about. "Have you seen any military?"

With a sharp barking laugh, which he immediately muffled by putting his dirty hand over his mouth, he whispered hoarsely, "You. I've seen you."

"And no one else in uniform?"

The man shook his head, and then turned and pulled the metal lid slowly down over his head. "Go away. You can't save us."

He was still over five miles from where he should find the precinct. The man hadn't told him much more than he already knew, but he was now confident he'd made the right decision to find Jo. Nowhere was safe, not the base, not the precinct and not the streets. According to the man in the dumpster, bullets didn't kill the creatures these people had become. There was no military presence in the city. Hundreds of thousands of people were dead. He couldn't leave Jo trapped in the precinct, and he set off at a steady pace.

The precinct was a good distance from the center of the city, and the further he travelled the flatter and less congested the area became. He trailed along Coors Boulevard, which was a six-lane highway with malls, shops and car yards on either side. In the distance on his right were low mountains, and it was eerily quiet. The wide road was jammed with vehicles, and many had large pools of blood inside them. The parking lots at each mall were half-empty, and he wondered if anyone was hiding inside them. If he hadn't been alone he might have stopped to investigate, but as it was there was nothing he could do to help anyone even if he found them.

While he trotted as quietly as he could along the road, he noticed black bodies dotted across one of the emptier parking lots. Behind the bodies was a two-story mall with a small entrance leading inside. Wanting to see his new enemy up close, he jogged to the right and across the scrubby border into the parking lot. The black body closest to him was wearing jeans, but the upper torso was black and half its head was missing. Quickly glancing around the area, and seeing no movement, he ran at a low crouch towards the prone body. Dropping to one knee, he peered curiously at the corpse.

Not wanting to touch the creature, although he was wearing assault gloves, he pulled his KABAR from his belt, and prodded at its exposed abdomen with the tip of his blade. The remaining flesh around blackened area was drained of blood, and was mostly skin and hardened fat. When he scraped the knife under it, it easily lifted away, exposing more of the blackened rubber. Scanning along the body, his eyes rested on its head. Something had blasted away half the face and skull, and the interior of its head was exposed. At first glance it looked as if it was a solid lump of black rubber, but he jabbed at the center with his blade, and it slid inside a softer mass. Now leaning closer, he continued to dig into the softer tissue, fascinated by the change in texture. It appeared, deep inside the core of what had once been the brain, was a tiny softer area made of a reddish tissue. If this was all that was left of the brain, then it would explain why the headshot had killed it. With its tiny brain buried so deeply inside the hard rubber, it would be a tough shot to make. He wanted to confirm his assessment, and looked around the parking lot for another body with a head wound. Finally standing up again, he was scanning the area when a low whistle caught his attention. The sound was coming from above him, and he looked up with his gun trained on the roofline.

A man's head appeared over the top of the roof and he waved. "Are you the army?" The man asked in a low voice.

In the silence around him, the man's voice travelled clearly, and he noticed the long nose of a rifle against the ledge of the roof. Judging by the number of corpses in the parking lot, the guy was a decent shot, and if he wanted to he could shoot him where he stood.

"No, I'm heading to the precinct."

"There's no one there."

"How do you know that?"

"I been over there and it was empty. No cars, no nothin'."

"The Commander was there four hours ago."

The man stood higher on the roof. "I didn't go inside. It ain't safe in the buildings."

"I heard it's not safe outside either."

"Yep, it's a bit fucked all round."

"Did you see what happened?"

"People went nuts and started killin' one another. I got me some ammo and been up here ever since."

He glanced around the parking lot at the vehicles and then back at the man. "You should take one of these cars and head to Kirtland Air Force Base. People have been told to go there. They've got the weapons and equipment to protect you."

Sniffing derisively, the man looked across the horizon. "Nah, I don't think so. I got enough ammo and shit up here. I'll wait 'em out."

"What makes you think they're going to leave?"

The man shrugged his lean shoulders. "Makes sense, don't it. Once they've killed everyone they can find, they'll fuck off. What would they hang around for? I've already seen a bunch of 'em leavin'."

"Where'd they go?"

"Dunno. They was headin' west."

He'd offered the man the only option he had, but he didn't want any help, and nodding brusquely at him, he said, "Okay. Good luck."

Giving him a quick nod in return, the man slowly sunk below the roofline again. In his brief tour of the city, he already knew more than they'd known in the bunker. The situation was perilous, and people were desperately trying to survive in any way they could. Although the creatures had started as human, they'd clearly evolved into something very different. They were hard to kill, and it would take a talented marksman with a high caliber weapon to put them down. He doubted that anyone other than his most highly trained troops could make that shot with any confidence.

When he finally arrived outside the building, the name of the precinct was engraved over the large double doors. The street outside of the office was strewn with cars and corpses, but he'd grown used to the sight now and it failed to shock him. Judging by the congestion of crashed and abandoned cars, they would have to make their way out by foot. There was no way they could drive, and it made him wonder how they could transport a group of sick children out of the hospital.

Making his way up the concrete steps, he cautiously poked the nose of his M4A1 through the door. The blow against the back of his tactical vest caught him by surprise. Something was clinging to his back, and he instinctively slammed himself against the side of the door. Whatever was hanging onto him was forced from his back, and he swung around firing wildly as he did. He might have seen the dead creatures in the parking lot, but the thing confronting him was nothing like he expected. It was missing half its face, but judging by the long hair on one side, he assumed it was once a woman. Wearing blood drenched jeans, one track shoe, and missing its shirt, chunks of human flesh hung loosely from what was now a rubbery, black torso.

He was firing continuously at her head, but he was only managing to push the woman back down the steps. Movement caught his attention, and more half-human people were running towards him. If he couldn't kill this woman by firing directly at her, then he didn't rate his chances at being able to stop the others. Stepping backwards towards the still open door, he was caught by surprise again by something dragging him through the gap.

"Shut the damned door!"

Allowing his weapon to fall against the sling on his side, he helped the dark-haired woman heave the glass door closed. Hard, black bodies began throwing themselves against the glass, and he worried it could break. The woman slid a bar across the metal handles on the door, grabbed his arm, and began to run down the corridor in her stockinged feet.

"C'mon! We gotta go!"

Following her down the corridor, he shouted, "I'm Bill."

"I guessed," she panted.

Skidding on the marble floor, she dove into a doorway and scooted over a wide counter. Moving awkwardly in his combat gear and pack, he followed her, and then saw where she was leading them. The precinct armory had their weapons stored behind a thick chain link metal barrier. There were no weapons left, but boxes of ammo were still scattered across the metal shelves.

"That's not a good idea. We'll be trapped."

Throwing herself through the door of the fenced wall, she shouted, "We're trapped anyway! It's this or die."

He wasn't sure he agreed with her summary of their situation, but he didn't know where else to run. Following her into the large armory filled with shelving, he slammed the door closed behind them.

"Now what?" He asked.

Pulling him deeper into the empty armory, she replied, "We wait. If we're lucky they won't find us." To his surprise, her face then broke into a wide smile, and she stuck out her hand. "Hi Bill, I'm Jo."

CHAPTER EIGHTEEN:
Witch under the bed (Dayton)

He'd left the six children with the woman he'd met on the oncology ward. Her name was Rosa and she worked for one of the pharmaceutical suppliers. She'd been on one of her routine visits promoting their drugs when the hospital had erupted into violence. Typical of a drug rep, she was immaculately dressed and groomed, but after hiding in the ceiling and then racing down the corridor with him, her hair was disheveled and her clothes were filthy and torn. Despite their dire situation, it amused him to see one of their usually perfect dealers looking worse for wear. The woman didn't seem to have an ounce of maternal instinct, and he was equally entertained watching her try and cope with six children. All of the kids suffered from long-term illnesses, which made them resilient, and he thought they were coping better than Rosa.

It had been six hours since he'd managed to talk to the woman at the precinct. She'd promised help was on its way, but no one had shown up, and the kids were thirsty and hungry. Since they'd found them in one of the wards, they'd managed to get them downstairs and had planned to leave the building. At the time it had been daylight and the hospital generators were still working, but now both had failed them. Hoping to get the kids some food and water, he was sneaking along the corridor outside the dispensary.

The reception area should have a flashlight, it was one of their emergency procedures, but the corridor was pitch black, and he was relying on his memory to find one of the tall counters. Using the wall as a guide, he was sliding his feet very slowly along the floor, trying to make as little noise as possible. The floor around him was cluttered with items he couldn't identify, and he tried to push them aside quietly. Whenever he heard the sound of high-pitched static squealing, he would pause and wait. When the noise subsided, he would continue his silent sliding along the wall. If he was lucky, he might find a service cart used to feed the patients, and as a last resort, he could find one of the medical staff rest rooms. There was always a fridge, coffee facilities and water cooler in them, and hopefully the food wouldn't be spoiled.

Running his fingers along the wall, only air remained, which meant he'd reached the end of the corridor. There would be a three-foot-wide gap between the wall and the tall counter. He slid around the corner, and slowly reached his hand out to where he should find the surface of the seating area behind the desk. Touching the smooth wooden desk, he began to run his hands gently over the surface. The flashlight should be tucked away behind the flat screen monitor. Using his hands to feel for the monitor, he ran one behind the screen, and found a tall, cylindrical object he assumed was the flashlight. It was one of the few times he was grateful for the pedantic nature of his profession. They were always told there would be a flashlight kept there, and sure enough there was one.

He hadn't thought beyond the problem of being able to see, but holding the heavy flashlight in his hand, he hesitated to flick it on. Emergencies didn't only happen during working hours, and there was never a time when the hospital was shut down, it was always busy at every hour of the day. Now without power or patients, it was strangely still, and sound was echoing down the corridors in a way he'd never heard before. Standing in the pitch black, he had no idea what was around him. Slight breezes were moving past him, but he wasn't sure if it was due to movement in the corridor, or there was an open window somewhere. The moment he flicked the switch on the flashlight he would be able to see and be seen.

When he was a young boy, he'd been frightened of a witch under his bed. He thought she could grab his feet and drag him under the bed, and being tall for his age didn't help. He had no idea why he thought she was there, but to avoid any chance of his toes dangling over the edge, he would bend his knees and curl into a fetal position. Unlike many children, he'd preferred to deal with her alone, and he hadn't shared his fear with anyone. If he was going to have a fight with a witch, then he'd sort her out on his own. Around that age, he'd also seen a horror film where red eyes had peered through a dark window, and it had made him paranoid about open curtains at night. Stuck in an isolated area of the family's large home, he'd always secured his curtains so no sign of the night beyond was visible, and slept like a baby curled up in the womb.

Holding the flashlight steady, he continued to blink his eyes at the blackness, as if that would help him see in the inky dark. Eventually he gave up and decided whatever was in the dark, he was just as prepared to fight it now as he had been when he was eight years old. Not wanting to be trapped behind the tall counter, he silently felt his way around the desk, until he was on the other side of the reception area and standing in the corridor.

Tensing and preparing to run, he flicked the flashlight on, and the corridor lit up sharply. It took a moment for his eyes to adjust, and he quickly absorbed the chaos down the corridor. Equipment, bodies, medical supplies and papers were scattered between the wide walls. Doors were open and wires were hanging down from the ceiling. He'd seen enough, and he flicked the flashlight off, quickly moving to the opposite wall to an open door. As he did, something brushed against him, skimming him lightly. A high-pitched squeal with a background noise of static filled the corridor, and he ducked behind the wall of the room.

While it continued to squeal angrily in the darkness, it moved along the corridor, disrupting the scattered items. As an oncologist and a surgeon, he'd learned how to force himself to remain calm under pressure. The creature was looking for him, but it didn't know where he was, and he held his ground. With his back against the wall, he held the flashlight with both hands, and gently bowed his head and waited. His heart rate remained steady, and found the place inside his head that was always calm and held onto it. Thanks to his job, he and death were old friends. At least half of his patients eventually died, and often the best he could offer them was a little more time to settle up. Some of them died filled with fear and anxiety, but others would go quietly into the night. It was those people he admired the most, and over the years he'd tried to learn the secret of their peace. They had a faith and acceptance of themselves and their lives. Through them, he'd learned to live his life honestly and to be the person he truly was, always finding something to be happy about each day.

The noise in the corridor subsided, as whatever it was left the area. It was probably still looking for him, but he needed to make his way to the next level. His memory was excellent, and he had only to be shown something once to remember it as a detailed picture in his mind. Now knowing what was in the corridor, he headed to the stairs at the end. When he bumped into something soft, he now knew it was a body. When he felt something solid, he knew it was equipment. At the stairs, he flicked his flashlight on again, and once the image of the bodies and papers had burned into his mind, he turned it off and headed up the stairs.

He'd worked at the hospital for seven years, and the layout was as familiar to him as his own home. On this level he would find several operating theaters and a refreshment area for surgeons and their staff. In retrospect, he suspected he spent more time at the hospital than anywhere else in his life. He supposed he could have gotten married and had children, and he probably still would. There was a part of him that resisted allowing anyone else into his life. Maybe his patients needed everything he had to give, and until he was confident he could take care of them, he didn't want the additional overhead of a family.

Edging along the corridor, he knew there was a door that would lead him into an operating theater. If he cut through the theater, he would find another door that would take him to a small preparation room. On the other side of that room was an even smaller area with a bed and a fridge. It was used for quick rest periods and was always stocked, but being the size of a large closet it wasn't used much.

The heavy doors of the theater room swung open slowly, and once they closed behind him, he flicked his flashlight on again. What he saw surprised him. The heavy metal table in the middle of the room was surrounded by equipment he recognized, but what was lying on the bed didn't make any sense. Leaving his flashlight on, he moved to the bed and played the light across the body on the table. The smell of rotting flesh washed over him. The face was clogged with breathing apparatus, and a sanitized disposable blue cloth had been draped across its hips and legs, but the abdomen and chest were open. Various metal instruments were pinned to the blackened, rubbery flesh, leaving the entire chest and gut exposed. He should have seen organs, fat and bone, but instead there was a gaping black hole. The patient must have died on the table, but their body was no longer human. Picking up an abandoned scalpel from a tray nearby, he prodded at the black surface of the wound. It was hard and solid like the tires on a car. Leaning closer, he sniffed at the hole, and it stank of burned rubber and putrid flesh.

Placing the flashlight so it lit up the man's head, he pulled the tubes from his withered mouth, and the skin pulled away. Similar to peeling an orange, the man's face rolled back over his head, still attached to the plastic tubing. Undeterred, he scraped away the last of the skin, revealing a pitch black face with a small round opening at the mouth. He prodded the scalpel into the man's nostrils, but they were sealed. Pushing the skin away from the side of his head, he prodded at the indentations where the ear holes should have been, but they were also closed. Like a petrified mummy, the man's black eyes appeared to be closed, but when he dug the scalpel into them, it became obvious the man had no eyelids.

He looked around the operating table until he found a pair of gloves and pulled them on. With his hands protected, he grabbed the man's arms and began to pull at the flesh. The rotting, soft skin sloughed away, and a black skinny arm appeared. Holding the man's arm firmly, he tugged the skin down until it slid over his hand, revealing black, thin fingers with large joints. Determined to understand the full nature of the change, he ripped away the blue cloth covering the man's lower body. He was naked underneath the sheet, and his skin was pale with blue botches. Screwing up his face in disgust, he began to pull and peel the skin from the man's hips and thighs. When he was done, all that remained was a sexless, black, rubbery looking creature. The joints were large and rounded compared to its skinny limbs. Featureless and barely creased, the creature looked like a molded doll. He knew it had once been a man, but nothing about it looked even remotely human now.

The body was hard and impenetrable, and it made him wonder how it could be killed. It didn't seem to have any internal organs. As a final act, he stabbed it with his scalpel and the blade snapped. Whatever these creatures were, it wasn't going to be easy to kill them. It was only then he realized they were trapped in a building full of monsters just like the one in front of him, and even if help was coming, he wasn't sure what they could do.

CHAPTER NINETEEN:
Last man standing
(Leon)

Their next landing wasn't as bad as their last, but the base was in chaos. Civilians were standing or sitting along the roads and between the buildings. Men and women in uniform were rushing across the base, and near the main gate four trucks were being loaded with weapons and other gear. There didn't seem to be enough people in uniform compared to the civilians, and he wondered where the army were.

Walking across the tarmac with Tuck, Lexie, Donna and the soldier they'd met on the plane, he was greeted by a Staff Sergeant. "Get to the trucks. You're heading into the city."

With that abrupt command, the Staff Sergeant saw something he didn't like, and stalked away shouting orders.

"What the hell...?" Tuck muttered.

He'd lost his pack and his gun at the last base, and hoping to replace his kit, he walked across to the trucks being loaded. Lexie was carrying her heavy boxes and she asked, "Do you think we can take one of the trucks to CaliTech?"

"I doubt it," he replied. "I'm guessing they're earmarked to go into the city." Stopping, he grabbed her armored arm. "You should come with us."

"Why?"

The soldier they'd met on the plane was listening to them. For some reason his nickname was Trigger, but he hadn't had time to ask why. Trigger leaned into Lexie's visor and said sternly, "Because you can help us deal with the bad guys."

With the added strength her hydraulics gave her, she pushed Trigger away and he lurched sharply. "Firstly, I'm not trained to deal with anything other than the gear. Secondly, you were the one that said you needed more of this kit and it's in CaliTech. And, thirdly, I don't work for you, so piss off."

She'd saved his ass twice now and he was grateful, but her attitude was getting on his nerves. She didn't seem to want to get involved, and yet she was part of the situation whether she liked it or not. Grabbing her arm more firmly, he said, "Cut it out, Lexie." Waving his arm at the frantic activity at the base, he said angrily, "All hell has broken loose and you are where you are. There are civilians in the city that need our help. You're coming with us, and when we get back we'll talk to command about going to CaliTech."

"What command?" She asked in disgust.

Soldiers in less than perfect combat gear were loading ammo and other kit into the trucks. There should have been more than one Sergeant shouting at them to get it right, but other than the large Staff Sergeant, they seemed to be working without direction. Lexie was probably right, and there was no one senior enough to command the base.

Turning back to her and seeing his face in her visor, he thought he looked washed out and tired. Trying to not to let his frustration show, he replied firmly, "Whoever's most senior is in command."

Lexie snorted. "Given the state of this place, that could well be you."

He was only a Staff Sergeant himself, and in army terms that put him pretty close to the bottom of the totem pole. If he was ever put in charge of a base, it would mean the entire country had fallen. The thought of being in command made him smirk, and he replied with genuine warmth, "C'mon. We need to join one of the trucks going to the city. You can bitch at me all the way there and all the way back."

While she walked with him towards the truck, she complained, "I'm not bitching. I'm raising valid issues. Don't invalidate me."

Rolling his eyes, he looked at Trigger walking by his side. "She's actually not too shabby in combat, but she does like to bitch."

Trigger gave Lexie a sidelong look and nodded. "As long as she can bring it, then she can bitch as much as she likes."

"I'm not getting any respect," Lexie complained loudly.

"You don't expect any, which is why you moan so much," Donna replied dourly.

Flicking Donna a grin, he was starting to understand how Lexie ticked. Her constant complaints were just her way of letting off steam. She'd complain and they'd ignore her, but when the fight started she'd kick ass. He decided it was an attitude he could work with, and walked over to the truck with the least number of soldiers loading it.

He called to the woman standing on top of the truck, "Staff Sergeant told us to join one of the trucks."

The woman looked up from the gun she was working on. "Who's the ninja?"

"New tech we're testing."

"Does it work?"

"Well enough, but it bitches a lot. Just ignore it."

"Nice introduction, dipshit," Lexie muttered.

Giving her a broad grin that he wasn't sure she could see through her visor, he replied, "Just telling it like it is. You should come with a health warning." The squad of three were heaving crates of ammo into the truck, and he pointed at the remaining boxes. "Make yourself useful and help us load this gear."

While Lexie easily lifted the heavy crates, he spoke to the woman on the top of the truck. "Who's in command?"

The woman gave a sharp laugh. "It wouldn't help to know. Our COs keep dropping like flies."

"What do you mean?"

"They either turn into homicidal maniacs or are killed by one."

"So, who's ordered us into the city?"

The woman shrugged. "There was some order from one of the government bunkers, but I dunno who gave the order or what happened to the CO who got it."

"What's happened in the city?"

She shrugged again. "According to the civvies who've made it out the place is a mess. Dead bodies everywhere. People have turned into killing machines and are murdering anyone they can find."

"Are the killers still in the city?"

"Guess so."

"Great. We've been ordered into a city full of killers."

"Oh, it gets better than that," another voice chimed in. "They're almost impossible to kill."

"Yeah, we know. It's fifty cal or above."

"Yep, and that's what we're packin'," the man replied. Waving his hand at the gun in the turret on the MaxxPro armored truck, he added, "That's an M2."

The 'Ma Deuce', as it was fondly called, was a .50-cal machine gun usually used by a gunner in the turret. It could fire single shots or forty rounds per minute. At a push it could fire eight hundred rounds in a minute, but that would burn through the ammo and wear out the gun. It was a fairly flexible weapon in that it could be mounted in the turret or used as a standalone weapon. Nodding at the man, he stepped forward into the MaxxPro, and saw several Barrett Sniper Rifles plus a Desert Eagle next to neatly piled boxes of .50-cal ammo. He'd lost his pack and weapons on the previous flight, and he eyed the Desert Eagle with interest. It was a big handgun, and like a S&W 500 Magnum revolver, it fired .50-cal rounds. Picking up the Desert Eagle, he nodded to himself and decided he'd just found his new favorite handgun.

The woman working on the Ma Deuce seemed to be in charge of the squad, and he liked the way she was thinking. Stepping back from the truck, he looked up at the woman and asked, "What are we supposed to do in the city?"

"Get a sit rep. This is a recon."

"And who are we gonna report it to?" He asked in surprise.

"Whoever's in charge when we get back," the woman replied firmly. Climbing down from the top of the truck, she winked at him and said, "I'm Sergeant Jenna Carter. I was put on lead...unless you want the job."

"No thanks. I'll manage the nav," he replied dourly.

"Is that what they call the tech?"

"Yeah, when we're done here, we need to get her to Johnsondale in California where there's more of it."

The Staff Sergeant came to talk to them while they were preparing to leave. He didn't have much to add to their orders, other than to tell them to kick ass and come back alive. It seemed they had a patchy line to one of the bunkers, and they were asking for a situation report about the city. The Staff Sergeant was staying at the base to continue to sort out civilians and supplies. According to him, people had been told to make their way to the base, but he wasn't sure why. It didn't look like they had anywhere near a full complement of troops, and there was no guarantee the people wouldn't turn into killers. He really didn't understand why anyone would think it was any safer at the base than anywhere else. When he asked Lexie if she could see anyone green through her visor, she'd shrugged and said there were too many people clustered together to be sure.

Once they'd finished their hasty preparation, he was relieved to leave the base. It was a sprawling site next to the Albuquerque International Airport, with a wide range of buildings and winding roads. There was no way they could secure the base in any decent way, and with the thousands of people already there, it was a question of time before some would turn and all hell would break loose. The city wouldn't be safe either, but for some reason he felt better when they were moving. At the very least they could drive away from the creatures, but it was a bad day when retreat was the only way to defend yourself, and it went against everything he was trained to do.

CHAPTER TWENTY:
Sight to behold
(Lexie)

This was only her second real combat mission. If she counted the landing at the base, then she supposed she could call it her third. She and Ark had done plenty of simulated missions together, but it was very different. Although their trials had emulated the actions of war, they didn't have the same edge of reality. During the trials she was prone to getting confused and stopping, which made Ark bark at her like a drill sergeant. She found his shouting alarming, and it had the desired effect of making her do as he instructed without any thought. Despite his bullying in combat, he was also the guy who would read to her until she fell asleep after a hard day of training. Since working with Ark she'd missed her sister less, and wondered if she was just too busy, or perhaps he was helping to fill the gap in her life. Being blind made it difficult for her to get close to people, and it took a long time for her to feel comfortable with anyone. She wasn't romantically involved with Ark, and he hadn't even made a pass at her, but he was slowly penetrating her defenses by being steady and reliable.

The equipment in the armored vehicle could interfere with her visor, so she was sitting on top of the truck as it rumbled down the road. Having been completely blind all of her life, she had no benchmark to compare the visor vision to actual sight. It was still a pleasure to see anything at all, and she was looking around the city with interest. They were passing two and three story buildings on the outskirts of the city, and the roads were becoming increasingly congested. Lumpy, grey outlines littered the streets, and she realized they were corpses. They emitted no active signal and were like any other inanimate object to her. Deep inside the buildings she detected life forms, which glowed a pinkish color indicating they were alive. There were also green blobs, and she knew they were the people who'd changed or were about to. Sometimes the green and pinkish blobs were together, and she wondered if those people knew they were with the killers. Plenty of weapons were being highlighted as well, and sometimes there were so many that the red outlines around the weapons overlapped, making a mad spiral of layered circles. Occasionally she saw the sharp lights of gunfire, and assumed there was a fight going on inside the building.

Donna had given Leon and Tuck spare radio earpieces so they could talk to her, and both men had joined the grid. There was a lot of chatter on the grid, and listening to it she finally understood the seriousness of their situation. The attacks were not an isolated issue, and it seemed every city had come under the same type of assault from their own citizens. According to Ark, CaliTech was in lockdown, and they had seven Navigators secured onsite, while everyone waited to be told what to do next.

The grid wasn't connected to the military comms system and she could only hear what Leon or Tuck were saying. It seemed they were heading for a police precinct called Northwest Area Command, but when Leon asked why, she couldn't hear what he was told through his military radio. She supposed it didn't really matter to her where they went in the city as long as they went to CaliTech once they were done. Her power packs would only last so long and her gear had weaknesses. She wanted to talk to the techs about replacement kit and replenish her power packs. They could be charged using standard power outlets, but she was worried what she would do if the electricity around her failed. Given the land and mobile phone lines were being lost, it was only a question of time before the power also completely failed.

"Keep scanning, Two One," Ark ordered.

"Spinning my head like a top is making me dizzy."

"I'm recording what the visor is picking up. We'll analyze the detail we're getting later."

"It's pretty interesting, Lex." Through the comms screen on her visor she knew Tank was talking to her.

"But you said you went outside with Amber to get her family."

"I did, Lex, but she lives in the 'burbs. It wasn't anywhere near as interesting as the city."

She didn't think the city was interesting. It was full of corpses, and although the others might not be able to see it from inside the truck, her visor showed an endless horizon of motionless bodies both on the streets and in the buildings.

"Were there as many dead people?" She asked unhappily.

Clearly listening to their conversation, Tuck remarked dourly, "The city is gonna become a health hazard."

"Is that your only concern?" She asked in horror at his casual attitude.

"Of course not," Tuck replied sharply. "I'm just looking ahead. These bodies will rot unless they're cleared, and the city will become uninhabitable."

"Both of you cut it out," Leon interrupted. "We'll deal with one problem at a time, and right now we're looking for anyone alive."

"There's plenty of people alive," she replied. "They're in the buildings, but so are the green blobs."

"We need a better name than 'green blobs'," Ark remarked.

"What we really need is to get the living out of the buildings and to the base," Leon replied. "Now I get why they sent the people there. No one can stay here. The city is lost."

"Is that what you're planning to do? Get all the people out of the buildings?" She asked.

"It would take a considerable force to get them out, and I'm not sure we have one," Leon replied bluntly.

While they'd been talking, the truck had weaved its way through the crashed and abandoned cars, and was stopped outside the white concrete stairs of what she assumed was the police precinct.

"What can you see, Lexie?" Leon asked.

She couldn't see any signs of human life, but there were nearly half a dozen green blobs clustered together on the ground floor. "Nothing much, just some green guys on the ground floor."

"Hang on, Two One, there's something deep inside the building. Zoom in," Ark ordered.

Obediently doing as she was asked, several pinkish blobs appeared, but there was some interference from the weapons and ammo being circled. Tapping her invisible screen to remove the weapons and ammo, the two bodies became clearer. "Oh, wait, there's a couple of people in there near the green guys. The green guys are grouped together."

"Maybe the people are hiding from them?" Leon suggested.

Zooming closer to view the moving forms, she and Ark tried to understand what they were seeing. "Is that a wall?" She asked uncertainly.

"Looks more like a gate."

"Why would there be a gate inside a building?"

"I dunno, but it looks like a barrier of some sort. It's probably the only thing keeping the green guys away from them."

"Okay, so we've got a front entrance, and they're about twenty yards down the corridor."

"There's an exit at the end of the corridor, but it's closed," Ark added.

Leon had been listening to them and said, "Okay, let me relay that to my guys and we'll work out how we can break in."

"We're going to break in?" She asked in surprise. "Why would you break in here and ignore all the people in the other buildings."

"Someone in there spoke to the bunker and that's where we're getting our orders from."

"Sounds like favoritism to me."

While she listened to one half of the conversation Leon had with the squad, it became apparent she was going to break into the building with them. Combat engagement number four was imminent and she wasn't looking forward to it. She didn't know what she was doing, and expected it would disintegrate into Ark barking and her doing as she was told. When Leon came back on her radio, he confirmed her suspicions, and she steeled herself for another fight. Always conscious of her blindness, her parents had treated her with gentle guidance and very little discipline. At the time they'd frustrated her, but now she felt ill-equipped to deal with the harshness of the real world, and she was missing their endless patience. Her irritable nature and sharp tongue usually kept most people at arms-length, but the army types weren't even slightly phased, and they seemed more amused by her than intimidated.

Taking a deep breath, she checked her power pack status and ammo. "This sucks," she muttered.

Leon led the squad of four to the front door, and they ran in a low crouch with their guns aimed, watching for movement that she could see without even trying. Sighing loudly, she dropped from the top of the truck. "There's nothing out here...yet."

Once outside the door, Leon said, "When you open the door, fire down the corridor. We've only got two sniper rifles firing fifty cals, so the rest of us can only hold them back with our M4s while we get inside. The two people are in a room approximately twenty yards down on the left. We need to get in and get them out." Batting her shoulder, he added, "Lexie, kill anything that comes for us."

"There's more of the green guys around and your shooting is gonna bring them to us," she replied unhappily.

"We know. We'll get the people out and let the trucks get us the hell outta here."

They couldn't see she was tensing inside her armor. Even with the hydraulics, the armor needed muscle to move it. The joints in the gear matched her own, but she still had to use her body to make it move in the ways she needed. It was one of the reasons the kit came with a small oxygen pipe. The cardio demands were beyond normal human ability, and after some of the Navigators had fainted with the effort, they'd taught them how to use the oxygen tank. Her tank was only half-full, and she prepared to sprint down the corridor, hoping they wouldn't shoot her. Anything less than a .50-cal wouldn't penetrate her armor, but it would hurt and it could leave her badly bruised.

One of the squad opened the door and her visor lit up with the gunfire. The green blobs separated and then began to run down the corridor. One was immediately hit with .50-cal bullets and it collapsed. The remaining four continued to fight against the bullets, but were being pushed backwards. The four squad members moved into the foyer and continued to fire.

"Ceasefire."

"Go, Two One."

As soon as they stopped firing, the green blobs launched down the corridor and she ran at them. Her own guns were less than .50-cal and they wouldn't do anything to the advancing blobs. When the first of them reached her, she grabbed it by the torso, and used it as a battering ram against the blob behind it. Both blobs merged into a single large green mass on her visor. Treating it like a rag doll, she pummeled it into the body of the one behind it. It fought back by pushing its arms against her chest plate, and kicking at her wildly. Another blob was trying to sidle past her in the corridor. Still holding onto the other one, she lunged and grabbed it by the head, then she stopped, unsure what to do with the three creatures she was holding back.

Ark's angry voice roared in her ears. "Break their legs!"

She wasn't sure how to do that, and instinctively lifted the one she had by the head high, and then slammed it into the hard floor. It seemed to crumple into itself and she let go of its head. Without waiting to see if it would rise again, she leaned down and grabbed the leg of the other blob. Pulling it by the leg until it was dangling upside down, she kicked at the blob behind it. With a force of over two thousand psi, the creature flew down the corridor, slamming hard against the wall. Still holding the other blob by its leg, she used her other hand to grab it by its round knee and snapped the leg in two.

"Down! Now!"

Not understanding why she was doing it, she dropped to the floor, and her visor showed nothing other than the bright light of gunfire above her head. The two squad members were using the sniper rifles to blow the green blobs apart. As their body parts flew in the air, their green glow was lost and they landed as inanimate objects.

The pinkish bodies she knew to be her squad were clustered over her prone body. "Nicely done," Leon said, as he patted at her armor.

Flipping lightly to her feet, she looked around the corridor. Other than her own squad, nothing was moving or showing as alive to her. The other pinkish blobs were leaving the room they'd been hiding in, and she could hear Leon brusquely introducing himself.

"Gotta go, Lexie," Leon ordered.

Breathing deeply, she tried to calm her rattled nerves and followed them along the corridor. When they returned to the truck, the driver left the area immediately and Leon spoke to her again.

"We've picked up a Colonel Bill Ketcher. He wants us to head to the hospital. He's pretty impressed with your gear, Lexie, and he's agreed we need to get to CaliTech asap."

Still feeling adrenalin coursing through her, she snorted irritably. "I've been telling you that all along."

CHAPTER TWENTY-ONE:
Stepping up
(Jonesy)

"Who farted?"

"Nobody farted, George. Don't be rude. The smell is decaying bodies," an older woman replied amiably.

George and his wife, Rose, were sitting in the back of his Malibu, and they'd kept up a steady chatter of nonsense from the moment they'd left his apartment block. Without needing to look again, he knew they were sitting side by side as if they were on a Sunday drive. He'd never really spoken to either of them and now he knew why.

"World's gone to hell," George remarked dourly.

"Yes, it has, George."

He hadn't recovered from discovering his wife of thirty years as a monster. Ever since that moment, his life had become surreal, and he agreed with George that the world had gone to hell. Miranda was somewhere in Las Vegas, and had he been in a saner frame of mind, he would have been trying to work out how to find her. As it was, he and Jas were now escorting the seven people they'd found at his apartment block out of the city. Jas was following him in another car being driven by John.

In his rear mirror, he could see John was still navigating around another abandoned car.

Catching his eye in the rear vision mirror, Rose asked kindly, "Are you okay?"

"I don't really know. Nothing about this situation feels real."

Next to him, Clarissa said gently, "I'm sorry about your Jenny. She was a very kind woman, Jonesy. Try and forget what you saw and remember her as she really was."

"I'm worried about Miranda."

"She was such a sweet little girl," Rose said sadly.

"Why do you say was?"

Rose sighed deeply. "George is right. The world has gone to hell. You may never find her, and it'll probably be impossible to even look for her." He felt Rose's hand on his shoulder. "You need to worry about the people who are with you and still alive. Hopefully someone somewhere is taking care of her too."

There seemed to be even more corpses on the road than before, and he suspected Rose was right. Everything had collapsed around them, and it was unlikely he would make it to Las Vegas alive. Even if by some miracle he made it to Miranda's home, she probably wouldn't be there, and he'd be back where he started. Only a day or so earlier he could have called her on the phone, but his mobile phone was dead. He couldn't even raise an engaged tone when he dialed her number, and he assumed the network was completely down.

He was driving along Tijeras Avenue when he finally saw something other than their own car moving. It was a large, black SUV with darkened windows and it was driving towards them. Other than being dented it looked fairly new, and the car with John, Jas and the other three people slowly came to a stop behind him. There were vehicles on either side of their two cars, and the only way he could drive was forward, but he was blocked by the black SUV.

"What do we do?" Rose asked.

"Wait and see what they want."

The door to the black car opened and a young man wearing jeans and a t-shirt climbed out. Typical of the younger street crowd, the man's pants hung low on his hips, and he was pointing a Saturday Night Special at them. Judging by the careless way he was holding the gun, he wasn't experienced with the weapon. Taking his Glock from its holster on his hip, he held it low and waited to see what the young man would do.

"I can't reverse unless John does," he warned. "I need you to duck down in your seats."

"Are they going to shoot us?" Rose asked in a relaxed tone.

"They might," he replied equally as casually.

He felt his chair being moved from behind and George muttered, "World's gone to hell."

"Get outta the car!" The young man shouted.

Pressing the button to lower his window, he called, "What do you want?"

Another man was climbing out from the passenger side of the black SUV, and now he had two targets. In his decades on the streets, he'd grown familiar with every type of thug. These two were what he thought of as opportunists. They weren't inherently bad boys, but given the right circumstances, they were capable of terrible crimes if they thought they could benefit from them. The only thing stopping the young man from firing was the possibility there was something still to be gained from keeping them alive. Clearly growing confident by their lack of response, both men began to saunter towards their car. As quietly as he could, he pulled the handle on the car door to unlatch it, but didn't swing it open.

"Whatcha got in the car, old man?"

"Nothing you need."

"You dunno what I need," the young man called back with a wide smirk. "I kinda like that hot piece in the other car."

"Jonesy," Clarissa said in a low voice.

The young man was moving across to his side of the car. Once he had a clear shot of one, he could take out the other before they'd have time to react.

"Stay low," he said softly.

"What if there are more in the car?"

"Jas will cover me from the other car," he replied.

The young man had finally moved within an easy shot, and quickly raising his Glock, he fired directly into his chest. While the man was flung backwards, he pushed open his door, swinging one leg outside and standing up. Shooting across the roof of the car, he hit the other man in the chest. In his peripheral vision, another door was opening on the black SUV, and he swung his handgun ready to fire. He never got a chance to pull the trigger before an eruption of gunfire came from his right. Holes were punching through the heavy door of the SUV, and the windows exploded into a spray of shattered glass. The sound was deafening and he dropped to the ground.

When the firing stopped, he lifted his head until he could see over the hood of his car. To his surprise, a large sandy-colored armored vehicle, complete with goggled soldier, was stopped twenty yards away. Uniformed soldiers were hustling from the vehicle, and moving fast and low across the street towards them.

"Drop your weapon!"

He placed his Glock on the hood of his car and raised his hands. "I'm a cop."

Other than his bloodied blue shirt, he wasn't wearing his full uniform, and the man behind the gun and dark glasses looked him up and down suspiciously. "You gotta a badge?"

Slowly reaching into his pocket, he pulled out his badge and threw it onto the hood. The soldier glanced at it and asked, "What did you shoot 'em for?"

"They were gonna be trouble." Flicking his head at his two cars, he added, "I've got eight people in these cars, and all except one of them is over fifty."

The soldier straightened and asked in disbelief, "Where were you all? An old people's home?"

"Don't be cheeky, young man. I said over fifty, not over seventy."

"I'm over seventy," George called from the car.

An older man wearing fatigues walked across from what now looked like a convoy of army trucks, and with his tactical vest and helmet, he looked like the real deal. Giving him a stern look, the man said, "I'm Colonel Bill Ketcher. I take it you're heading out of the city."

"Yeah, I've been told to get people to the Kirtland Air Force Base."

It was then he saw Jo making her way across the intersection. Grinning widely, he lowered his arms. "Jo."

"Jonesy."

He didn't know her well enough to hug her, but after the past twenty-four hours, he wanted to. She stood awkwardly next to Bill, and he suspected she felt the same way. With neither of them able to breach the protocol of polite behavior, they simply stood staring at one another with matching wide smiles.

"You know one another?" Bill asked in surprise.

Still smiling at him, Jo replied, "Of course I do. He's one of my officers. He was the one that told me about the people tearing their faces off."

Bill gave him an appraising look and nodded. "Okay, I'm gonna have one of the trucks escort you out."

He shook his head. "I don't want to leave. I was just going to take these people to a clear road and let them drive themselves."

"What's your plan?" Jo asked.

Looking up at the buildings around them, he said, "There's people in all of these buildings. We need to help them leave."

As if to prove his point, several people appeared at one of the doors of a building. "Are you the army?"

Their voices carried across the road, and more people were leaving the buildings around them. Very quickly there were more than fifty people walking across the intersection. Glancing at Bill, he said, "This isn't safe."

"It's not safe anywhere." Speaking into his mike, Bill ordered, "Alpha and Delta, head to the hospital. We'll deal with these people."

"What's at the hospital?" He asked.

"Kids," Jo replied tersely. "I promised a doctor there we'd send help."

"Is there any help?" He asked doubtfully.

"Not really," Bill said. "This is kinda it right now."

"Then we need to keep people moving," he replied.

CHAPTER TWENTY-TWO:
Bolt hole in hell
(Leon)

"Okay, we've got our orders."

"But you don't even know that guy," Lexie complained.

Giving her a dour look, he replied, "I don't need to know him. He's a Colonel and now he's my CO."

"It's Armageddon, but you'll still do as you're told by some guy you don't know?"

"It's how the military works, Lexie."

The two trucks were weaving their way along the narrow and crowded streets, driving one behind the other. Inside his truck were a couple of soldiers he didn't know, Tuck, Jenna and Trigger. Lexie was on the roof of the truck, which he didn't like, but her gear was bulky and there wasn't much room inside. He'd never met the five troopers in the other truck that Bill was now calling Delta team. In typical fashion of an officer, Bill had climbed into their truck, immediately commandeered their radios and starting issuing orders. Despite assuring Lexie this was how the system worked, he wasn't entirely sure he had to do what anyone told him anymore. Every base he'd been to on their long journey home was in chaos, and he wasn't convinced there was any viable military left standing. Old habits die hard, and he figured he would do as Bill ordered until he was convinced there was a reason not to.

Trigger gave him a quizzical look, and guessing he wanted to know what they were talking about, he said, "She doesn't understand why we're following the Colonel's orders."

"She has a point," Trigger remarked. "For all we know that guy just found a uniform."

"Nah," Jenna replied decisively. "He had brass attitude."

He didn't doubt Bill was who he said he was, but Trigger was right, and in the current situation they couldn't be sure. "We'll call it on a case by case basis. But there are kids in that hospital and I'd get them out, with or without being ordered to."

"You've got a death wish," Lexie said dourly.

"It's not a death wish. I've had this job for eight years, and if anyone has the skills to get those kids out then it's us, so that's what we're gonna do."

Lexie snorted. "Fine, but I really need to get to CaliTech."

"What's she talking about?" Trigger asked.

"She wants to go to CaliTech. They're the company that designed and built the gear she's wearing."

"Then she's right, we need more of it."

Lexie must have overheard Trigger through his radio mike and she replied, "Finally somebody with a brain."

He was about to object when the truck came to a stop, and he peered through the narrow opening assuming they were at the hospital. If they were, then he couldn't see any building that looked like one.

"Why are we stopping?"

"People ahead," the driver replied steadily.

He asked, "Lexie, what do you see?"

"Lotsa pink blobs."

Frustrated, he looked at Jenna and she shrugged and pointed to the door. He supposed they would need to find out what was going on. Opening the door to the truck, he cautiously poked his gun outside. It was then he heard the voices.

"Are you army?"

"Help us."

"We need to get out."

"You need to get us outta here!"

Stepping out of the truck, he was confronted by at least fifty people standing between them and the abandoned vehicles on the road. He glanced up at the tall buildings surrounding them and decided it was too dangerous to be stopped on the street. Looking across at Lexie, who was still sitting on top of the truck, he said, "Lexie, get down here."

"Why? There's fifty people out here and we can't help them. They need to get back into the buildings and find somewhere safe. There's critters in the buildings and they're already heading towards the exits."

"You coulda mentioned that earlier. Now, get down here and lead these people wherever it's safe."

Lexie jumped down from the roof of the truck. "Like where, Leon? Where is safe? Every building has critters."

A flare of irritation flashed through him and he said firmly, "Then we'll go in with them and make it safe."

"I thought we were rescuing kids at the hospital?"

Before he could tell her to stop wasting time, he heard Ark's calm voice through his radio. "This is how combat works, Lexie. Things change and you deal with each problem as it happens. Right now we have to get these people secured, so let's do that."

"But if we stop for every group looking for help, then we'll never make it to the hospital."

Ark's voice became soothing. "It's okay, just follow your orders. You think too much, Lexie. We'll deal with this problem and then the next one, until eventually we run out of problems. Stop thinking and just do, it'll be fine."

Other than knowing how to use the sophisticated gear, it was becoming obvious to him that Lexie didn't have a clue what she was doing. Ark was right, she needed to do as she was told, and that's what he was politely telling her.

His point wasn't missed by Lexie. "In other words shut up and do as I'm told."

"Yes, ma'am," Ark replied.

He couldn't see her shrug under the heavy armor, but her tone was one of resignation. "Fine, then their best bet is the small supermarket. It has food and a storage room at the back with no windows."

Scanning the line of buildings, there was a small supermarket with a green awning. The front entrance had a wide glass door, and flyers offering discounts were still pinned to the windows. Past the painted signs and flyers on the window, the supermarket looked fairly undisturbed, and he was surprised it hadn't been raided. The people on the street were beginning to gather around his open truck door, and dressed in everything from jeans to business wear, they all looked tired and frightened. He noticed several children and a few teenagers in the group forming around him, and some of the people were clearly injured, making him wonder how they'd survived their attackers.

It had clearly been a long few days in the city, but he waved their questions away. "I dunno about that, Lexie, there's at least fifty of them."

"No, she's right," Ark replied. "They'll need food and water."

"But what if some of them turn?"

"With fifty people at least it'll be a fair fight," Ark replied flatly.

"Nothing about this is fair," he replied dourly. Turning to face the crowd, he said loudly, "Okay, folks, we don't have the transport or support to take you out of the city. You can make your own way out and head to Kirtland Air Force Base, or we'll get you secured inside the supermarket. It has food and water and you can hide in the storage room."

"Where's the army?" A man asked.

He shook his head. "We're only the recon troops. The rest are...back at the base."

"What are they doing there? Why aren't they here killing these things?"

He couldn't see much point to lying. "We've had the same problems on the bases that you've had in the city. Our people have been turning as well."

"Are you saying there's no army?" A woman asked in horror. "Who's going to get us out of here?"

Lexie saved him having to answer, and through his headset he heard her speak. "They're coming in force."

"Lock the trucks down!" He began pushing the people in front of him, herding them towards the supermarket and its cheerful green awning. "Go! Go! Go! They're coming." Through his radio, he shouted, "Hold 'em back, Lexie."

"No need to shout. I'm blind, not deaf," she muttered, as she swiftly climbed to the top of the truck.

He didn't have time to watch what she was doing and assumed Ark would guide her. He didn't know much about the tech, but he was starting to understand why there was a shadow nav. With their advanced vision, they could defend themselves from threats others couldn't see, but it was a lot of data to absorb and process. Behind him the gunners had opened fire, and he guessed the critters, as Lexie had just named them, were already on the street. Not bothering to look, he continued to push the people in the direction of the supermarket, and Jenna and Trigger were herding even more people towards the entrance.

When he reached the wide single door, he realized he didn't know what was inside and called, "Ark! What's it like in there?"

"Kinda busy, Leon, but there were at least two of them."

Trigger appeared at his side. "What's the status?"

He didn't know Trigger and he wished Tuck was with him. "Two in the shop."

Trigger called. "Jenna, open the door and we'll go in."

He had an M4 and the Desert Eagle, but only the handgun was .50-cal and able to take down the critters. With only a seven round magazine, he'd need to make every shot count. "Are you crazy?"

Grinning widely, Trigger pulled a sawed-off shotgun from his pack in a fluid movement. "Some say I am, but I say I gotta shotgun."

Smirking, he asked, "Do you think that'll work?"

Shrugging, Trigger replied, "Let's find out."

It was a risky maneuver, but life had just gotten a lot more dangerous and he shrugged in reply. Raising his Desert Eagle with both hands, Jenna opened the door and he cautiously walked into the supermarket. With the power off, the shop was gloomy, but he could see shelves of food and a cashier counter to his left. Trigger had followed him into the shop, and they both stood about six yards apart, peering down the narrow aisles.

"What do you think?" He asked.

"I'll lead, you follow. We'll cover one another to reload."

That made sense to him. "Roger that."

Trigger walked ahead of him, swinging his head and shotgun from left to right. When they were half way down the fifteen-yard long aisle, a high pitch static screeching broke out to his left. He pointed his gun in the direction of the noise, and was rewarded by the sight of a black-faced critter still wearing remnants of its clothing and skin. It seemed to bounce across the top of the shelves, and he opened fire at it just as it was about to jump into their aisle. With its rapid movement, the shot went wild, and he now had six rounds left in the gun.

Trigger aimed his shotgun directly at the critter. "Stand clear."

At such close quarters, he was at risk of being hit by buckshot, and he pulled back, crashing into the shelves behind him. The sound of the shotgun exploded in his ears, and he instinctively ducked. A spray of black rubber fell on the floor in front of him, and he felt it landing on his helmet. Quickly looking up, there was another critter running across the top of the shelves towards them. It seemed oblivious to the fate of its brother, and he aimed his gun at it. This time he was able to see the impact of the Desert Eagle. The critter's head had literally vaporized with the blast, and its body collapsed into the next aisle.

"Ark, are we clear now?" He didn't get a reply immediately and asked, "Ark?"

"Still kinda busy, Leon, but yeah, the site looks good to go."

He had no idea what was going on outside and called, "Jenna, get them in here."

People began to run past him in the narrow aisle, grabbing food from the shelves as they went. "Secure any doors at the back," he called.

It wasn't a great solution, but it would have to do for now. Forcing his way past the heaving movement around him, he found Jenna at the door. "What's going on out there?"

"Crap. Lexie and the gunners have been killing the creatures, but there's only so much they can do. There's too many of them."

He batted Jenna on the arm. "Then we gotta go."

He, Jenna and Trigger ran to their truck and were joined by Tuck and the other two soldiers. Scattered across the cars and road were half human and half black, rubbery bodies.

"Where have you been?" He asked Tuck.

"I could ask you the same question."

Weighed down by their gear, they clambered into the truck and he asked, "Where's Lexie?"

"Don't worry about her," Ark replied. "She'll find you."

The driver had kept the engine idling and both vehicles began to slowly move along the road. Through the narrow slit in the truck, he could see more critters were running from the buildings. Suddenly his view was blocked by the now familiar black armor. Lexie was running alongside their truck, and he was surprised at how relieved he was to see her. Clearly she wasn't a soldier, but she never shirked a fight, and he respected her cojones in combat.

"That was not a solution," Jenna said unhappily.

Leaving fifty men, women and children holed up inside a storage room didn't solve their problem, and he wasn't happy either. "I know, but it's all we can do for now."

CHAPTER TWENTY-THREE:
Lemmings
(Lexie)

After securing the fifty or so people in the supermarket, she was again sitting on top of the truck with the gunner, when the large, squat hospital building came into view. The hospital was surrounded by a collection of pale colored buildings, and there was an open concrete area in front of the main doors. Through her visor, she could see inanimate human shaped lumps on the ground, and wondered whether they were critters or people. She suspected, had she been able to see them properly, the number of dead bodies inside the buildings and on the road would have been overwhelming. As it was, the corpses were only inanimate objects in her visor, something to step over and nothing to do with her. Using the zoom and detail function on her visor, she was able to locate the living in the buildings around her, but they were often surrounded by the ominous green blobs she was now calling critters. It was their movement that made her think of critters. The blobs were fast and scuttled about, often on four or more legs.

No one seemed to grasp her need to get back to CaliTech. She couldn't make them understand the tech didn't maintain itself and she needed more kit and power. Ark had told her CaliTech was under lockdown and no one was allowed to enter or leave. Amber had snuck out with Tank to get her husband and two kids, but when the Chief Executive had found out he'd almost refused to let them back inside, and if he hadn't needed both of them he might not have. Being lowly ranked in the company, she didn't know the Chief Executive, Duncan Liederman, but Ark assured her that he was an asshole.

"Lexie, pay attention. I need you to recon the hospital," Ark said through her earpiece.

"I don't even know what that means."

"Get off the truck and move around the perimeter of the hospital with your visor on detail scan."

Providing she looked at what Ark needed to see, they would be able zoom in on the interior of the hospital and identify where the people and the critters were. It would give the soldiers a fighting chance, and she dropped from the roof of the truck. Knowing Leon could hear what Ark had just said to her, she began to run lightly up the stairs to the hospital entrance. She could see through the walls of the building and there were plenty of critters inside. The place was a mess, and there were overturned tables and chairs scattered across the wide seating area at the front of the building.

One of the advantages of her armor and strength was she could barge through pretty much anything, and she began to run along the glass front of the hospital until it became a solid wall. Her visor had cameras able to capture anything three hundred and sixty degrees around her, plus another set of cameras capturing images above her head. The wide vision available through her helmet made it impossible to make sense of everything she was capable of seeing, which was why the shadow nav was essential. Ark would be working with the other shadow navs to analyze the images and identify targets, risks and civilians. She was basically a vaguely intelligent robot, and used to gather information other people would analyze.

Through her earpiece she heard Ark beginning to brief the combat team still secured in the trucks. "You've got about twenty enemies on the ground floor."

Wanting to feel useful, she interrupted, "Critters. I call them critters."

Ark ignored her interruption and continued, "Okay, we're seeing some people in the middle of the ground floor. It looks like two adults and maybe six smaller bodies, which I assume are the kids."

"What are the upper floors looking like?" Leon asked.

"We've got less visibility of the upper floors, so it's harder to tell. I can get Two One to check it out if you need more detail."

"Gee, thanks, Ark," she replied sarcastically. For Leon's benefit she added, "That means he'll tell me to go to the upper floors to take a look."

Through her radio she heard Leon having a one sided conversation. "There's about twenty critters on the ground floor, and two adults and six kids." Leon paused and then said, "I don't want us going into the building without any idea what's above us. Twenty enemy is bad enough. We haven't got a chance of getting out alive with any more." After a longer pause, Leon said, "Yeah, okay, I'll tell Ark."

She had no idea what they were planning to do, but then Leon said, "Ark, send her in and tell her to stop anymore critters coming to the ground floor."

"Did you get that, Two One?" Ark asked.

Pleased that Leon had adopted her name for the green blobs, she asked cheekily, "Do I work for both of you idiots now?"

In unison, both Ark and Leon replied sharply, "Yes."

The military types could be very funny when they chose to be, but when it came to who worked for who and obeying orders, they were ridiculously serious. She'd completed her circuit of the hospital, jumping walls when she needed to, and was again standing on the steps leading to the entrance. She looked up at the roof over the front steps, and figured she could probably jump onto it and smash her way into the second floor. The critters hadn't been able to penetrate her armor, and with her hydraulics, she was probably stronger than they were. Having handled a few of them, they seemed to bend in ways that a human shouldn't, but they didn't survive having their limbs and heads torn off.

Using the power of her hydraulic knee joints, she launched from a standing position to a beam attached to the overhanging roof. Learning how to move in the gear hadn't been easy, but it came naturally to her now. It required a combination of using her muscles, and then relying on the hydraulics to add to her movement. It meant she could run faster and leap higher than was naturally possible. From her vantage point on the roof, she scanned the interior of the second floor of the building. Leon was right to worry about the critters on the upper floors. There were at least another fifty on the second level, and they were moving sluggishly around the rooms.

"There are two entrances to the ground floor. One is at the back and I think they can secure that one. The other one is the main stairwell to the reception area. You'll need to stop anything from getting down those stairs," Ark informed her.

"Maybe she can draw the critters on the ground floor to the next level." Leon suggested.

"That's a better idea," Ark replied. "Two One, go through the front entrance on the ground floor. Once they're on your tail you can lead them upstairs."

"She'll need to be careful they don't overwhelm her," Leon said.

It was nice someone was considering her welfare and she replied, "Thank you, Leon. I'm glad someone cares about my ass."

"I care about your ass, Two One, it's a nice ass and I'd hate to lose it," Ark replied cheekily.

"I hate both of you," she replied, as she dropped from the roof over the entrance and prepared to enter the glass doors.

The wide glass doors should have opened automatically, but clearly the power was off. Wedging her thick gloves in the crack between the doors, she easily pushed them open. She was met by another set of identical glass doors and opened those next. The generous foyer was filled with rows of chairs bolted to the floor and a large reception desk. Her movement had attracted the attention of the critters, and they were already moving towards her. One hurtled down a corridor and then ran across the floor in her direction. It was quickly joined by more green blobs charging at her position. Through her visor she could see some of the critters hadn't reacted to her entrance, and she began to run towards a corridor leading to them.

Making as much noise as she could, there were now a dozen or more critters on her tail. Her helmet muted most sound, but the high-pitched screeching penetrated her earpieces.

"Head for the main stairs," Ark ordered.

Running the circuit of corridors, she barged back into the reception area and began to run up the stairs. More critters from the second floor were already making their way down the stairs, and she grabbed several by the throat, smashing their heads into the stairs. The critters were tough, but even they didn't survive the impact of having their heads crushed on impact. As soon as they were killed, their bodies lost any sign of life, and her visor saw them as inanimate objects. At least fifteen of the critters were following her up the stairs, and she assumed the squad would be entering the hospital, but she didn't have time to use the detail scan on her visor to find out.

Reaching the top of the stairs, she found herself the focus of the attention of a large number of critters. At least ten of them were heading down the corridor towards her, and she aggressively leapt forward.

"That's good, Two One, but not too fast, they need to keep up with you," Ark said calmly.

Her instinct was to run like maniac down the long corridor, but she slowed her pace. "Easy for you to say."

"You're doing fine," Ark replied steadily. "I can see some more people in the rooms on this floor and above. We'll get them later."

"How?"

"We'll get who we can get and then reconvene."

A cluster of green blobs appeared in front of her, but there were so many she couldn't tell how many critters there were. Her visor filled with green and she threw her arms around wildly. Her guns were less than .50-cal and firing at them wouldn't do her any good. Grunting with the effort, she continued to bash wildly at the green light that was filling her vision.

"Stay close to the stairs, Two One, you need to stop them from getting down there."

Continuing to punch wildly, she clutched at anything she could get her hands around. She had something in her hand, and she jerked sharply, hoping to tear the limb from its owner. Feeling it come loose, she dropped it and punched out again. Through her thick armor, she could feel the pressure of the bodies against her. Crouching low, she burst upwards, allowing herself to spring into the air and then drop again much like a wrestler. Her weight, combined with gravity, crushed the critters she landed on.

Through her earpiece, she could hear Ark talking to the squad, but she was too busy attacking the green blobs around her to listen. He would tell her when to leave, and in the meantime she would just have to survive. More weight continued to press against her and she was starting to feel overwhelmed. Talking to her onboard computer, she said curtly, "Air.". Her order would release oxygen into her helmet to boost her flagging energy. If she fainted the critters would crush her, and she was relying on the oxygen to keep her alert.

She didn't stop moving and ripping at the critters that were now on every side of her. Her breath was becoming ragged and she was feeling slightly dizzy with the continuous effort. The critters weren't giving up, but neither was she. Ark was clearly monitoring her condition and said, "We need to pull Two One out. There's too many of them. She can't maintain the pace."

"Lexie, get out!" Leon called.

Quickly moving to top of the stairs, her vision briefly cleared, and she saw a group of people running towards the main entrance. The critters would follow her if she went down the stairs, and there was no way they could get out of the building fast enough before they would be on top of them. She needed to lead them away from the escaping people.

There was another large room to her right. The door was closed, but she assumed it would give if she hit it hard enough. Using her shoulder to barge through the door, it crashed open and she ran across the room, heading for a window on the far right of the building. The critters seemed to be excited by the chase, and they followed her into the room. She could run faster than the critters, but she wanted them on her tail and slowed slightly so they could keep up. The window was looming in her visor, and on the other side were rows of parked cars. If she crashed through the window, she would drop two floors onto the roof of a car. Although the armor protected her from bullets and the hydraulics gave her strength, she could still injure herself if she landed badly.

The cameras could be damaged more readily than the rest of her, and she'd been taught not to use her helmet like a battering ram. Leaping the last five feet at the window, she twisted her body so her shoulder armor took the brunt of crashing through the glass. Flying through the air, she tried to keep body twisted to land on her side. Her shoulder hit the roof of a car, and she tipped herself onto her back, skidding from the roof and onto the trunk of the vehicle. Backflipping untidily, she felt critters thud against her body, as they followed her course out of the hospital. Some of the critters had clearly landed badly, but others were already stumbling to their feet.

The critters were obviously pretty stupid. They'd followed her out of the hospital completely unaware they would fall, possibly to their deaths. The realization gave her and idea and she said, "I'm going back in."

"Two One, report back to the trucks," Ark said sternly.

"I'm going to run through every level and lead the critters to the roof."

"I like it," Leon said. "We'll head upstairs and grab anyone left alive."

"Nice plan, Leon, but how does Two One get down from the roof?" Ark asked. "There's a limit to how many critters she can deal with."

"I'll climb down."

"You'll break your legs if you fall."

While she continued to argue with Ark, she was already making her way up the stairs towards the second level.

Flicking her lower face helmet up, she began to hoot loudly. The sound of her voice was attracting the critters, and she continued to climb the stairs to the next level.

Through her mike she heard Leon shouting, "Go! Go! Go!"

Her visor was filling with green again and she shouted, "Ark, I can't see!"

"Straight ahead, Two One."

His steady voice guided her to climb one set of stairs after another. Bodies were pressing against her, and she used the maximum strength on her hydraulics to push through them. It was like walking through treacle, and her body was being pushed from all directions, effectively holding her in position. Her power was dropping rapidly, and she felt a familiar surge of panic.

"Last set of stairs, Two One. Keep fighting. There's a door in front of you."

Her heavily gloved hands felt the door, and she used her full strength to push against it. The door snapped open and she burst onto the roof of the building. There were no critters in front of her, and her vision cleared. The roof had a number of outlined boxes, and she ran forward hoping to find a way down. Critters were following her, and she stood on the edge of the roof desperately looking for a way to escape. During her training, they'd taught her how to make her way down a flat surface using ropes, but she didn't have any now. The critters had followed her onto the roof, and they were forming an impenetrable wall behind her. As they surged forward, they would push her over the ledge. Realizing she would have to improvise, she dropped from the wall, relying on the hydraulics in her gloves to hold onto the ledge with her hands. Critters were stupidly following her, and were falling the five floors to the ground.

"Let go," Ark said sharply.

"Are freaking serious?" She asked in alarm.

"Grab anything you can as you slide. It'll slow you down."

"That's your plan?" She asked in disbelief.

"No, Two One, this was your plan. You really shouldn't be allowed out on your own, but you're here now, so let go."

"Do it, Lexie," Leon said. "You've got no other choice."

"I hate both of you," she said grimly as she let go of the ledge.

Her body slid down the wall, and she pushed her hands against it hoping to find anything she could hold onto. She could feel the toes of her boots riding over bumps against the wall. When her fingers felt anything, she bent them sharply and her descent was slowed, but she was still gaining speed. Her body began to pull away from the wall, and hoping she was now only three floors from the ground, she kicked fiercely against it. The kick pushed her away from the wall and she was flying through the air. She had no idea what she would land on, and twisted her body so her shoulder would take the impact. Landing with a loud crunch, she was sure she'd broken something in her hydraulics, and she skidded on what turned out to be grass. Rolling herself onto her back, she held her arms and legs above the ground until she stopped.

"You okay?" Leon asked worriedly.

Warning signals were flashing on her visor, and it seemed her onboard computer was very upset with her. Nothing hurt, but something was definitely very broken.

"Yeah, but I think I just wrecked my gear."

Struggling to stand, she realized her left arm hydraulics weren't working anymore. Staggering to her feet, she began to stumble towards the trucks.

"Hurry up, Lexie, we gotta go," Leon called.

Her hydraulics weren't responding properly. "I don't think I can run."

She limped over to the truck and the doors opened. A number of cars filled with people were driving in a line between the two armored trucks, and she assumed the squad had successfully retrieved anyone left alive in the hospital. Hands pulled her into the truck and she collapsed onto the floor. As the truck began to move, someone pulled her helmet from her face and she heard Leon speak.

"That was pretty stupid, Lexie. Awesome, but stupid."

CHAPTER TWENTY-FOUR:
No place to run
(Leon)

Compared to the fight in the hospital, the trip back to the base was uneventful. They were protecting ten cars with as many civilians as they could transport, and they couldn't stop to help anyone else. The city was a disaster. Some buildings were burning, people were trapped inside others, and the critters were everywhere. Even with Lexie acting as bait to lure the critters to the second floor, they'd used a lot of ammo rescuing the people from the hospital. The critters didn't die easily, and he wanted to get back to the relative safety of the base. He was worried about Amelia and his unborn son. She was in Seattle, some fifteen hundred miles from where he was now, and it was more than possible they were both dead. A numbness was settling over him, and he didn't know whether he was in shock, or simply too tired to feel anything.

The last time he'd slept was on the flight to the previous base, but it wasn't quality sleep. He could barely remember the last time he'd had a hot meal. They hadn't stopped moving from the moment Lexie had found them about to be executed in the desert. The time zone changes were confusing him, and he couldn't remember if it had been three or four days ago. Touching the now dirty bandage on his neck, he prodded the cut to assess how well it was healing.

Watching him poke at his wound, Donna said, "You should change that."

He didn't reply, but followed her into the briefing room with Trigger, Tuck, Lexie and several troopers he didn't know. The civilians they'd rescued had disappeared into the crowd of people now hanging around the base, and the doctor, who'd introduced himself as Dayton, had joined them in the meeting room. When he walked in, Bill and Jo were staring at a map on the wall, and they turned to watch them file into the room. Still dressed in his fatigues and armor, Bill cut a straight-backed, stocky shape, and judging by his salt and pepper hair and deeply lined face, he guessed the man was in his late forties. With his hand still pointing at a location on the map, he noted it had the squared look and stubby fingers of someone who'd done a lot of manual work. Despite his solid muscular look, he thought he could detect the slight swell of a paunch under the man's body armor. As was typical of many senior officers, Bill had clearly once been very fit, but was now sliding into middle age.

"Did you get it done?" Bill asked brusquely.

"Yes, sir," he replied.

Dayton pushed his way to the front of the room. "I'm Dayton. I worked at the hospital as an Oncologist."

Jo gave Dayton a tired smile. "I'm Jo. You spoke to me on the phone."

Dayton nodded gratefully. "Thank you."

"Don't thank me," Jo replied, with a small shake of her head.

Bill cut their conversation short. "It looks like people are turning and their primary intent is to kill us..."

"Critters," Lexie said decisively. "We're calling them critters."

Nodding curtly, Bill continued, "Fine, but they're hard to kill."

"Fifty cal or above," Trigger interrupted.

Bill gave Trigger a tired look. "The base isn't secure. We have tens of thousands of people here, but we don't know if they won't turn into...critters."

"Is there any command or government left?" He asked.

"None that we can rely on," Jo replied.

Bill nodded again. "She's right. We don't know who will turn or when. It means we've got no stable leadership or troops."

"I've spoken to Central Command at CaliTech. They have access to satellite images, and they said they saw a huge number of people in the desert," Donna said.

"What were they doing there?" He asked.

Bill replied, "We don't know, but I'd like to find out." Everyone looked at Bill and he added firmly, "These critters are doing the same thing by killing everyone and that implies they're organized. If there's a large group of people in the desert, I'm willing to bet they're not human."

Frowning, he said, "That means they're in the city and the desert. Why would they cluster in those two locations?"

"Maybe the ones in the city just haven't made it to the desert yet, or maybe they don't know to go to the desert," Jo suggested.

"We need more information," Bill said confidently. Nodding at him and Jenna, he added, "You need to check it out. Take the nav with you."

"I have a name," Lexie said dourly. "And I have no hydraulics."

Giving Lexie a concerned look, Bill asked, "What happened?"

"I fell off a building. It was Ark's idea."

"No, it wasn't, Lexie," Donna said bluntly. "I was on the grid while you were at the hospital. What you did was really dumb. You're lucky you aren't dead."

He wasn't really listening to their argument, but was watching Bill intently. He'd just told them there was no army and no command structure. With what he'd seen in the city, it would take an army to clear it, but it didn't look like they had one. It made him wonder why he didn't just leave. Amelia could still be alive, in which case he should look for her. The chances of him surviving the fifteen-hundred-mile trip weren't good, and the thought of even trying made him look across at Lexie. If he had a Navigator with him, or better still if he could use the gear himself, he might have a chance of surviving the journey.

Bill seemed to read his mind. "Don't even think about it, Sergeant."

"I have a family," he replied.

"You also have a duty," Bill countered.

Under the current circumstances, he didn't need Bill's permission to leave. He could slip away and no one would know where he went, or even if he was still alive. There was no need to argue his case with Bill and he shrugged at his comment.

"I need to get back to CaliTech in California," Lexie said irritably. "Now my gear is fried I don't have a choice, and neither do you if you want to use me."

He'd either need one of the Navigators or their gear to make it to Seattle, so now he wanted to go to CaliTech as badly as Lexie did. Batting her arm, he said firmly, "So, let's go."

"What? Now?" She replied in surprise.

In a tone that made it clear it wasn't a request, Bill said, "If you're going to CaliTech, then I want you to check out that desert location."

He wasn't used to questioning his orders in front of his superiors, and he gave Bill a skeptical look, but said nothing. Seeing his expression, Bill said, "Look, we have an enemy, and the more you know about your enemy, the better your chances are of defeating them." Giving him a steely glare, he added, "I can't make you follow my orders, but if you want to survive then you need to use your head, and not just your firepower."

He glanced at Tuck who was lounging against the wall. In response to his unspoken question, Tuck gave a slight shrug. In that one gesture, he knew Tuck would support whatever decision he made. He needed Lexie to guide them to CaliTech, and even without her hydraulics, she could still identify the critters through her visor.

"What do you think, Lexie?"

"About what?"

"Will you take us to CaliTech?"

"Sure, but Ark wants me to check out the desert on the way there."

"Why?"

"He says if they're critters, then we need to know what they're doing."

Lexie seemed to do whatever Ark told her, which meant he was going to the desert whether he wanted to or not. Nodding to Bill, he said, "Guess we're going to the desert, but then we have to go to CaliTech. We need their navs and the gear."

"Good enough. Get back here when you're done," Bill replied. Clearly seeing his doubtful expression, he added, "There's vehicles, weapons and supplies here, plus I need a briefing about what you find."

He nodded and left the room with Trigger, Lexie, Tuck and Donna. Once they were out of earshot, Tuck asked, "Did you just emancipate us?"

Trigger snorted. "Of course he didn't. There's nothing left to emancipate ourselves from."

Standing outside the building, he stared across the parking lot and surrounding land. There were people wandering or sitting everywhere. Many were covered in bloodstains, all looked shocked, and there was nothing anyone could do to help them. Clearly they'd already broken into the supplies held at the base, and MRE's, bottles of water and military packs were scattered everywhere. Some people had put up makeshift tents, and others were starting small fires. Cars and other military vehicles were parked haphazardly wherever anyone had thought to stop. Their own trucks were still guarded by the troops they'd returned with. It looked as if they'd refilled the gas tanks and had scrounged more ammo and supplies. Jenna seemed to be running the show and he walked across to her.

"The Colonel wants us to go to the desert on the way to CaliTech. What do you want to do?"

Giving him a weary look, she replied, "I don't know. I had family in Chicago, but I doubt they're still there or even alive."

"We can't stay here," Tuck said decisively. He pointedly surveyed the battered-looking people and added, "Any one of them could turn on us."

Lexie and Donna had joined them, and they formed a small circle, each staring intently over the others in front of them. Instinctively they were forming a perimeter, and he realized they couldn't stay at the base. For as committed as he had been to his job, he didn't have one anymore. If the government and military were gone, then it was every man for himself. Looking at Jenna, he figured she had the trust of the seven men and women still reloading the two trucks with whatever they could find.

Flicking his head at the busy troopers, he asked Jenna, "Are they with you?"

Jenna shook her head slowly. "Only inasmuch as they've no one else to follow, but once they realize no one's in command then maybe not."

He really needed the gear at CaliTech, and nodding at her, he said, "Come with us. We'll do what the Colonel asks only because Ark at CaliTech wants the data as well. Then we'll head to CaliTech. Ark says it's a secured site, plus the navs can see the critters through their visors."

She nodded back at him. "Sounds like a plan."

CHAPTER TWENTY-FIVE:
Moving on
(Bill)

"That didn't go well," Jo said, as she watched them walking across the parking lot at the base.

"No, it didn't."

In some ways, he didn't blame them. He had his own family to consider. Although his father had died several years earlier, his mother was still very much alive in Boston. He did have a wife, but she'd divorced him after she learned about his affair with a civilian he'd met while he was stationed in Germany. His wife had waited until the girls were eighteen before filing for divorce. He'd come back from a deployment to find the house empty, except for their divorce papers and a pen on the kitchen counter. She'd courteously left him a brief note explaining she'd known about his affair for several years, and now their daughters were old enough, she was done with him. It wasn't his proudest moment, and his two daughters wouldn't talk to him anymore. They were both in their twenties and he had no idea where they lived now. Apparently he wasn't allowed to make even one mistake in his life, and he'd never spoken to her or the girls again.

Since his divorce, he'd lived alone and moved from one command to the next. He supposed that's why they'd made him a liaison for the bunkers. With so little family, his loyalties weren't split, but the bunkers were a disaster. They'd always assumed they'd be able to communicate with the surface, and there'd be some structure left after any disaster.

"What now?" Jo asked.

Staring out of the window, the squad he'd sent to the hospital were finishing loading their trucks, and he didn't blame them for wanting to leave immediately. The base wasn't secure. Under Jo's direction, civilians had flooded into the base and had broken into the supplies. Guns, ammo, food, and other survival gear had been raided and there wasn't much left. The soldiers on the base were scarce, and many had already left to look for their families. With no command structure, the base had disintegrated into chaos. It made him wonder what had happened to USNORTHCOM. They should have been providing military support for the civilian authorities. It was possible their bunker was operational, but they'd been unable to find any military command topside. NORAD was in control of the nukes and should be managing the satellites. If they went to DEFCON 1, then they'd start firing the nukes, but he had no idea what they'd target. He could try and make his way to their bunker, but even if he got there, there was no way he could gain access or make any difference.

Dayton hadn't left with the others, and he joined them staring out of the window. "I want to go back to the city."

"What for?" Jo asked in surprise.

"I have a theory, but I need the equipment at the hospital to test it."

"What's your theory?" He asked.

"I found a dead one in the hospital. It must have turned while it was being operated on and it died on the table. It was solid...by that I mean it didn't have any organs that I could see. It's like a thick, black rubbery creature. Its joints might look human, but they bend in ways they shouldn't. It didn't have any sexual organs, so I don't know how they reproduce."

"Do they need to?" Jo asked. "It seems to me they reproduce by taking over humans."

Dayton nodded enthusiastically. "Exactly. I don't think they need to reproduce...they're relying on us to do it for them."

Puzzled by the man's gleeful observation, he asked, "And that's good because...?"

"It means they need us, so they can't kill us all," Dayton replied. "I also noticed they don't have mandibles or a functioning jaw. Their mouths appear to be a slit or a hole, but I don't know how they use it."

"Have you seen one eat?" He asked Jo.

She shook her head and Dayton continued, "I never got a chance to scan one and I need to. You said we need to know more about them and we do. If I can get a generator working, then I can use the equipment at the hospital to do some analysis."

"The city isn't safe."

Dayton gave him a look of disbelief. "Nowhere is safe. If I'm going to die, then I can't think of a better place than at my hospital. It's kinda where I live anyway."

The squad had clearly decided there was nothing for them at the base, and they were already driving away from the building. The whole area was filled with waiting people, and while he watched, they slowly navigated their way along the crowded road.

Still watching the squad leave, he said distractedly, "Missiles. We need missiles."

"What for?" Jo asked, sounding surprised. "What would we bomb?"

He wasn't really sure. Even if they bombed their own cities, it wouldn't stop more people from turning into critters. The real problem was they were their own enemy. Even now, he wasn't sure who would become his enemy.

"Air support," he muttered. "We need better visibility."

"Oh well, if you're just compiling a wish list, then I'd like to be on an island...alone," Jo replied dourly.

"Can you get me a ride back into the city?" Dayton asked.

Jo nodded. "Jonesy and another cop stayed. They were on Tijeras Avenue and Fourth Street last time I saw them. If we can hook you up with them, maybe they can help you get something working at the hospital." Touching his arm, and with a look of genuine concern, she added, "But you're also a doctor, and there's a lot of people here who need help."

Dayton shook his head firmly. "No, we have to get to the source of the problem, and I can't do that here."

He'd been taught how to analyze combat situations and command troops, but right now he didn't have enough information and no troops. When confronted with a problem with no apparent solution, he'd been taught to break it down, which was what he was trying to do now. As part of his training, he'd been told not to assume anything, and that made him wonder why the cities hadn't been completely taken over. According to his debriefing, the buildings were full of people and critters, and he wondered how any people were surviving at all. The critters were hard to kill, and not too many civilians had .50-cal weapons.

"Why isn't everyone dead in the city?" He asked.

"What sort of question is that?" Jo asked.

"No, he's right," Dayton agreed. "When I was trapped in the dispensary at the hospital, I kept waiting for them to attack and they didn't. They could have found us, but they never really looked."

"Maybe they're stupid or you got lucky," Jo suggested.

He shook his head. "No, that's not it. There's people and critters in all the buildings. They could wipe out everyone if they wanted to. They've done enough to break us, but not enough to wipe us out. It doesn't make sense."

"What? Do you think there's a master plan?" Jo asked in disbelief.

Her question made him realize that was exactly what he thought. To successfully wipe out the government, military and emergency command structures was either the luckiest strike he'd ever seen, or there was intelligence behind it. It would explain why they were gathering in the desert. They were forming their own bases and command structure. Continuing to watch the area outside the window, he thought their enemy would also need to stop them from forming any viable defense. The people standing and sitting around the base could be used at any time to form another army to attack them. It was then he realized they'd made a massive mistake.

"We need to get the people out of here," he said urgently.

"Why?" Jo asked. "They need our help."

"Because we won't be allowed to group together like this. They'll see it as a threat and infiltrate us. All they have to do is turn some of us into critters and then the killing starts."

"Who will do that?"

"Whoever it is that's done this. None of this is an accident, it's been too effective."

Jo closed her eyes, and he could see she was grasping his point. "So, what do we do?"

"Cells. We need to form small cells. That way, even if some people turn into critters, there's only so many people they can kill." Turning to Dayton, he added, "And you're right. You need to study them. I don't care where you do that, but share whatever you learn with whoever you can."

Whenever he was right about anything, a sense of confidence would flood through him, and he felt it now. They weren't fighting a mindless enemy, but an organized force. It led him to wonder why they were keeping some of them alive. They must have something the critters needed, but he didn't have enough information to know what it was. Watching the people wandering across the once organized base, he wondered how he could convince them to form into smaller groups. He needed to get Dayton back to the city and break up the base. Before he could issue any orders to anyone, a fight broke out amongst the crowd. There was a chance it was the result of frayed tempers, but more likely someone had turned and more would follow.

Turning and pushing Dayton and Jo toward the door, he said grimly, "We have to go."

CHAPTER TWENTY-SIX:
Bloodless coup
(Ark)

The Chief Executive had made one of his rare trips to the basement of the building and was eyeing their screens skeptically. His name was Duncan something or other, but he'd never bothered to remember the man's full name. Everyone simply called him Dunk the Skunk and it really did suit him. Despite his immaculately tailored suit and matching shirt, he still emanated an air of sleaziness more commonly found in a cheap strip joint. He could well imagine Dunk the Skunk leering at something, only he doubted the man was human enough to be attracted to an actual woman. He suspected the only thing Dunk ever coveted was money and power.

Right now, he was storming around their small space swearing about getting no respect. According to Dunk, he'd placed calls with people as high as the President, and no one was calling him back. In response, they'd called up the latest satellite pictures of the cities, and showed him they were burning and in chaos. This perfectly reasonable explanation had only enraged the skunk even further. Apparently, the demise of their country had been done just to annoy him.

"It's appalling! How dare they ignore me?"

"They're not ignoring you. They're dead," he replied amiably.

"How do you know that?" Dunk the Skunk asked contemptuously.

When Tank had returned from helping Amber bring her family back to the site, Dunk had collared him and was dragging him around like a disobedient puppy. Tank was still fully armored and his shoulder weapons were loaded. With his face helmet flipped up, he couldn't see his eyes behind the visor, but the straight line of his lips made it clear he was angry. Tank wasn't the kind of guy who was easily annoyed, nor was he the sort of man you wanted to get offside.

In response to Dunk's question, Dom had loaded more satellite images of corpses piled high in the streets of one of the cities. Flicking his thumb at the pictures, he said, "Because this is what's going on out there."

"They could be faked."

"Why would anybody fake that?" He asked in surprise.

"I've been out there, and believe me, they're faking nothing," Tank said bluntly.

Dunk whirled and glared at Tank. "I know what you've been doing and I'll deal with you later."

Tank had clearly reached his limit with being bullied, and calling him by a name that acknowledged their once common rank of Sergeant First Class, he said blandly. "Just say the word, Battle."

Without needing to be told, he knew Tank was prepared to put the man down and hold him by the throat. He was proposing a coup, and he had to admit he was tempted. Lexie and Donna were on their way to CaliTech with an armed squad, and once they arrived there was no way Dunk would be left in charge. It was only a question of whether he and Tank took control of the site now, or they waited for the squad to arrive.

Despite the obliqueness of Tank's offer, Dunk had finally sensed their collective mood towards him. Narrowing his eyes, he straightened his back and said angrily, "Don't even think about it."

Leaning back in his chair, he asked amiably, "Why not?" He waved his hands at the screens displaying the burning cities. "Think about it, Dunk. What if these pictures are real? What if the government has really fallen and there's no military left?"

Dunk replied sharply, "There's always military left. Even if you lose the troops, then the equipment and weapons are still around, and there's plenty of people who've been through the military who know how to use them."

"I think you're missing the point," he replied with slight shake of his head. "Think a little harder, Dunk. What could possibly have brought our country to its knees without firing a single weapon?" When Dunk didn't reply, he waggled his finger at him and added with a wink, "Now, that's one smart fuckin' enemy."

Finally, their situation seemed to be sinking in and Dunk asked, "Do you have any pictures of this enemy?"

"Yes and no," he replied.

In response to Dunk's question, Dom began to pull up short video displays of people being attacked. Most of the footage showed people attacking other people, and it looked like a savage one-sided bar brawl.

Dunk looked surprised. "Are you telling me we did this to ourselves?"

"I don't think so," he replied. Pointing at the screen next to him, he added grimly, "Watch this."

Dom had loaded the footage from Lexie's encounter at the hospital. Being blind and confined to her visor style vision, she couldn't see what the green blobs attacking her really looked like. Once she'd made it onto the roof, they'd managed to get images of the critters in clear daylight. The name critters made light of what was actually a terrifying new monster. Dom had slowed the speed of the footage as Lexie was bursting through the door on the roof. As she slowly made her way through the door and onto the roof, spindly legged, black rubbery creatures were following her. They moved in rapid jerking motions, scuttling slightly left and right as they propelled themselves forward.

Isolating several, Dom enlarged them on the screen. One had twenty skinny, knobby legs emerging from a fat rounded torso that was at least three feet wide. Its head was tiny in comparison to its body and no bigger than an orange. The other enlarged picture was that of a taller, more humanoid looking creature, but it had long spindly limbs with lethal claws at the end. Its head was more in proportion, but it had a spout with a hole in the end where its mouth should be. Even in the slightly blurry footage, something seemed to be dripping from the end of the spout, and he had a nasty suspicion it probably spat some sort of poison or acid.

While Lexie continued across the screen in slow motion, the creatures were following hard on her heels, almost on top of her and clawing wildly at the back of her armor. He wasn't confident she would have survived if they'd managed to overwhelm her, and he'd told her to jump from the building for good reason.

"What are they?" Dunk asked flatly.

"They were people, but I don't know what they are now."

"What the hell has happened?" Dunk asked, almost in disbelief.

"I think we've been invaded."

"By what?"

"A disease maybe. Something that's changing people into these monsters."

"How many people have changed," Dunk asked warily.

He shrugged. "Hard to say, but it's at least fifty percent of the population, plus it seems it can happen to anyone at any time." Giving him a friendly smirk, he added cheekily, "It could even happen to you."

"What's happened to Northern Command? Why haven't they issued orders to the Army? What about NORAD? If the satellites are still up, then they must be operational."

Shrugging again, he replied, "Maybe so, but they're not gonna talk to us. It's not like we can just phone them." Shaking his head, he added, "You're forgetting that anyone can turn. Why would anyone in the bunkers at NORAD or even Camp David be immune? The only reason we can protect CaliTech is because the visors can detect them. The first sign anyone else gets that someone has turned is when they try to kill them. Based on the images we've seen, every city has been hit, and something like half the people have turned into these freaks."

"Don't forget the ones that changed have killed a helluva lot of people as well," Tank added dourly.

Grinning at Tank, he replied, "True story."

Dunk glared at him. "Do you think this is funny?"

"Of course it isn't funny, but we're in the right place at the right time."

"How do you figure that?"

"Fifty cal weapons can kill them, plus the nav armor is effective and so are the hydraulics. We need to do a lot more testing, but there's an army squad on its way here now."

Dunk looked confused. "Why are the army coming here? I thought you said there was no army."

"There isn't, but we've got seven navs here trained to use the gear, plus the techs. We need to train more people, preferably ones with combat and weapons experience."

"And then what?"

Tank snorted. "Then we kick ass."

"I'm not handing my gear over to the army," Dunk replied in disgust.

"Why not?"

"They haven't paid for it."

He and Tank had talked it through. According to the inventory manifest, there were at least a thousand full sets of gear in the warehouse and a range of visors. Through the visors they could detect anyone who'd turned, and Navigators were already monitoring the staff on the site. Initially anyone who'd turned had been sent home, but now they were holding them in a secured building on the grounds. Since seeing the footage from the hospital, he now thought the small building was like a garden shed full of spiders. Tank had suggested they destroy the building, but he wanted to keep the critters. They could be used to analyze their enemy, so they could learn how to destroy them. Both he and Tank had agreed they could train the incoming squad, and then they would go into the cities and learn as much as they could. Providing at least one satellite stayed functional, they'd be able to get more footage of what was happening. Lexie was on her way to the desert location where they'd seen hundreds of thousands of people. The satellites might be orbiting, but they couldn't control them, and he needed her to take a look in person. They still didn't know what the people were doing there.

He and Tank had a plan, and he leaned back in his chair so he could look Dunk in the eye. "The situation has changed and this tech is needed. You can sort out the bill later."

"I'm not handing over billions of dollars in equipment and research to anyone without being paid," Dunk replied angrily. "It's taken me fifteen years to put this in place and I own it!"

"I'm sure you'll be paid very well once the problem is sorted, but right now there's no one to pay you."

"I don't care. The site is safe and we'll wait it out."

Tank was giving Dunk a grim look and had positioned himself behind him. They'd agreed they would ask first, but either way they would take control if Dunk wasn't cooperative.

"You need to see the bigger picture," he said amiably.

Quickly turning and seeing Tank behind him, Dunk asked, "Or what?"

"You know what." Spreading his hands in a reasonable gesture, he added, "Look, you can go back to your fancy office and leave this to us, or we can put you in the shed with all the other critters, but I don't rate your chances."

Whirling back to look at him in shock, Dunk asked angrily, "Are you threatening me?"

"No, I'm advising you."

Clearly Dunk hadn't built an empire by being a stupid man and his shoulders slumped. "Fine."

Without saying another word, Dunk walked to the door and Tank asked, "Should I let him go?"

He shrugged. "What can he do?"

"I think we should kill him."

"Other than being an asshole, he hasn't done anything wrong." Giving Tank a wry smile, he added, "But if he ever does, then you can kill him."

CHAPTER TWENTY-SEVEN:
Earth redefined
(Leon)

He still wasn't happy about his discussion with Bill and was trying to work out why. On the one hand, there was no army for him to report to, but old habits die hard. Bill was his commanding officer and he'd left the man with nothing.

The truck was bumping along the desert track and he asked Tuck, "Do you think we should have left like that?"

"We're following our orders."

"No, we're not. We only agreed to come here because Ark wants to know what's here. You and I both know that. I mean, who the hell are we working for?" Tuck shrugged and he continued. "If there's no army then I should be looking for Amelia in Seattle, not hacking around the desert."

"How are you gonna get to Seattle?"

"I dunno. We could just go there now."

Trigger kicked his boot. "No way, dude. We need that nav gear, otherwise we'd be fucked. And anyways, you're wrong about command."

"What do you mean?"

Leaning closer, Trigger replied, "The point of the military is to defend the country. We build weapons, train soldiers and have equipment for that one purpose. It's not the organization that counts, the important bit is the ability to defend our country. If what we've got doesn't do the job, then we find something that can. Improvise and adapt, dude. You know the drill."

He nodded. "I guess that's what we're doing."

"We're doing what we're trained to do. These fuckers are hardcore and we need better weapons."

Tuck nodded, and Jenna said through their radios. "We're about three miles from the last known position of the people. We should go by foot from here."

As the trucks came to a stop, he asked, "Lexie, what can you see?"

She was sitting next to Donna, still in her under gear, which consisted of the black webbing filled with wires and sensors, and her heavy boots looked enormous against her long, lean legs. She was still able to control the screens using the sensors in her gloves, and she began moving her hands rapidly across the air in front of her.

"Ark, what the hell is that?" Lexie asked.

Ark's calm voice spoke through his headset. "I don't know, but it looks like a lot of green lifeforms about a mile and a half north of you."

"What's your guess, Ark?" He asked.

"Tens of thousands of critters."

"Shiiit," Tuck said unnecessarily.

"What happened? Did all of the people turn?" He asked.

"I'm guessing so, but can you get Lexie closer so we can get some decent footage?"

"I have no armor or hydraulics, Ark. Do you wanna get me killed?" Lexie complained. "I thought you liked me."

"Stop whining, Two One," Ark replied sternly. "You have troopers with you. You'll be fine."

"You all suck."

Climbing out of the truck, he checked their weapons. They had two Barrett Sniper rifles, a Desert Eagle, Trigger had his sawed-off Mossberg shotgun, and Jenna had scrounged four M26 shotguns from the base. The gunners had M2 .50-cal machine guns mounted to the top of the trucks, but the .50-cal bullets were huge, and the gun and ammo were too heavy to carry across the desert. It meant they'd have to make every round count with the weapons they could carry, but he'd prefer to avoid any engagement. If there were as many critters there as Ark suspected, then they'd lose no matter how good their weapons were. They simply didn't have enough firepower, and he wished they could call in an airstrike.

"We can only arm six of us and still leave the two trucks defended, so only six of us can go," he said. "Jenna, stay with the trucks and deal with these guys."

Jenna nodded, and he turned to Tuck. "Trigger, Lexie, you and two others will recon the site with me."

It took them twenty minutes to load ammo and check one another's gear. There was very little cover in the desert, and he hoped they wouldn't have to get too close to the actual site. "Ark, how close do you need Lexie to be?"

"It depends on what's there. To see anything above ground, two hundred yards should be close enough to get a very detailed scan, but to see anything underground, she needs to be within at least fifty yards."

"Underground? Why would you need to see underground?"

"Last time we saw the site, there were about two hundred thousand people there, but I'm not seeing enough lifeforms for that."

"Maybe some of them died?"

"Maybe."

The trek across the desert was tedious. They were weighed down by their equipment, and Lexie was clumsy without her hydraulics. She was a slight woman under all the heavy gear she wore, and her body was lean thanks to the excessive cardio needed to run and leap in her armor. Half her face was hidden under the visor and her cropped blonde hair was plastered flat to her head. Watching her slide in the sand, he put his hand in the middle of her small back and pushed her forward. The loose sand was sitting on the surface of the harder ground beneath it, but it made it difficult to move at any speed. Next to where they were walking was a wide trampled area that looked like it could be easier to move on. Waving his hand at the squad, he indicated they should follow the path.

"What the hell caused this?" Tuck asked.

"Two hundred thousand people," Trigger replied.

Once they were on slightly firmer ground, they picked up their pace. They were less than half a mile from the cluster of green blobs Lexie could see through her visor, when Ark said, "You need to proceed with caution. There are lifeforms moving around half a mile ahead of you."

Waving to the squad, he said, "Tuck, Trigger, Lexie, you're with me." Nodding to the two troopers he didn't know, he added, "You two stay here and watch our six. Stay out of sight."

The other two troopers moved away from the battered path they were following, and set up the sniper rifle against a slope hidden by low, dry looking bushes. He and the others proceeded forward, holding their weapons ready to fire. Night was just beginning to fall, and the light around them was greying. On the more solid ground, Lexie was sure footed, but he was all too aware she was unarmed. He'd wanted to give her his Desert Eagle, but Ark had said no. Apparently her marksmanship was so poor, she was more likely to shoot them. He didn't like auto-targeting weapons, and had no doubt that was all Lexie could use.

Creeping forward as quickly and quietly as they could, he became aware of movement around them. They were two hundred yards from the site, when he stopped and indicated they all needed to get down. Flattened against the earth, he looked in disbelief at what was sitting in the middle of the desert. He was pretty sure it hadn't been there before, and it blended so well against the background, they were almost on it before they realized what it was. Rising out of the sand was a mound that peaked like a rounded pyramid. Amid the sandy walls, were dark holes, pitted in an almost organized way in rings around the mound. Even stranger, was the movement across the entire surface. It seemed to be humming with activity, and he realized black critters were running along the walls. He couldn't work out why they weren't falling down the hill the mound created. It had to be five hundred feet high, and a third of a mile around, making it roughly the size of a large pyramid. With its sharp sloping surface, gravity should have been pulling the critters to the ground, but instead they were clinging effortlessly, and sprinting nimbly along its walls.

"What the fuck is that?" Tuck whispered hoarsely.

Suddenly Lexie gave a sharp shriek and leapt to her feet. "Oh crap, they're everywhere!" She was dancing from foot to foot, as if trying to avoid any contact with the ground.

Launching to one knee, he grabbed her arm and pulled her to the ground again. "Shut up," he whispered urgently.

She twisted against his grip. "Let go of me."

"You need to get out right now," Ark said steadily.

Without questioning Ark, he immediately climbed to his feet. "Go. Go. Go."

As they began to back away from the mound, Ark said, "Go faster."

While he turned and broke into a run, he asked, "Why?"

He never heard Ark's answer, but the earth replied for him. Drilling its way from beneath their feet, a black creature covered in dirt and sand emerged. Trigger blew its head off with the shotgun before it had a chance to fully escape from its grave. In the dimming light, he could feel and see the hard earth moving around them.

Grabbing Lexie by the arm, he roared, "Run!"

Scattering along the wide path towards the other shooters, they all began to sprint. Hitting the fast release on his pack, he let it fall to the ground behind him. Tuck had Lexie by her other arm, and they both held onto her as they raced down the path. Tracer fire was lighting up around them, and he guessed the two shooters they'd left behind were covering their flight back to the trucks. He had the Desert Eagle and Tuck had an M26. They wouldn't have time to reload and he shouted, "Conserve your ammo."

In front of him, a critter was struggling to climb onto its spindly legs out of a hole in the ground, and he took aim with his Desert Eagle. The weapon had a real kick to it, and it wasn't the sort of gun you fired while running at full speed. He waited until they were almost on top of the creature, and fired a center mass shot. The bullet did its work and blasted its torso in half. The critter folded and they ran over the top of it.

Reaching the location where they'd left the other two shooters, he called, "Go! Go! Go!"

As he ran towards them, they were leaping to their feet to join them in their sprint. Just as one of them was grabbing the sniper rifle, a black critter leapt from a hole in the ground and dragged him down. Before he could raise his gun again, more critters leapt on the man, and he was buried under a frenzy of black movement.

"Keep going!" Trigger shouted from behind him.

He wanted to stop and help the guy, but Trigger was right, and he was most certainly dead. Even in the gloom, he could see more bursts of dirt erupting into the air as critters exploded from the ground. They were screwed. Without enough firepower, there was no way they could fight their way out. It was then he heard the distant sound of machine gun fire and it was coming closer. Ark must have talked to Jenna and sent her forward. He was really starting to like Jenna, the woman was reliable in a crisis.

They'd just run what he guessed was close to a six-minute mile, and his lungs were beginning to burn. He still had a firm grip on Lexie, and without the sandy surface, she was still running strongly.

"Trucks," he gasped.

Their vehicles came into sight and there was tracer fire in every direction. Now he was worried they might shoot them, and to make a smaller target, he called, "Single file."

Letting go of Lexie's arm, he pushed her forward towards the oncoming trucks. It took less than a minute for them to reach their position, and the gunners were keeping up a steady rate of fire. As he ran over to the truck, Jenna's squad were already pulling Lexie inside. Hitting the side of the truck, a critter launched itself onto the roof, swiping wildly at the gunner who immediately ducked down. Trigger appeared by his side, and grabbing a skinny leg each, they roughly yanked the creature down. While Trigger slammed his boot into the critter's abdomen, he fired another round into its head. The Desert Eagle bucked in his hand, and the sound reverberated against the side of the truck, but there was no head left.

The gunner had reappeared at his post, and they scrambled into the back of the truck, hearing the doors bang shut. The driver was turning in a wide arc to follow the path to leave. Even over the roar of the laboring engine, he could hear banging on the outside of the truck. Suddenly the gunner dropped inside and said, "Shit! Just go!"

"Man the gun," he said urgently.

The gunner gave him a look of horror. "I can't. Some of these fuckers are airborne."

He looked back at him in shock. "You've gotta be kidding me." Realizing he didn't need an answer, he said, "Get us outta here. Top speed." Lexie was still breathing heavily, and he grabbed her arm. "What do you see?"

"They're everywhere, in the air, topside and below."

"We have to get to CaliTech," he said grimly.

CHAPTER TWENTY-EIGHT:
Mankind redefined
(Jonesy)

He'd spent the morning looking for transport that he could use to get people out of the city safely. They needed guns and reinforced, reliable vehicles. Jas had suggested they use the fire trucks, but there were less of them, and they weren't designed to carry people. The Albuquerque police drove Dodge Chargers, and their distinctive black and white sides made them stand out. Cops were issued with Glock 17 or 19s, plus their vehicles should have Tasers or Remington 870 shotguns. If he was really lucky, he might even find a stash of personal weapons including AR-15s.

So far, they'd found two cop cars that were still working, plus they each had two shotguns. He had no idea where the police driving them had gone, but the blood in the passenger and driver's seat told its own story, so he didn't bother to think about it. He had thousands of people trapped in buildings surrounded by homicidal maniacs, only that title didn't suit them anymore. The black, rubbery creatures they'd turned into reminded him of insects and not humans. He and Jas had seen one that had twenty legs and a stumpy body. It had scuttled along, much like a cockroach, and had moved just as quickly. Typical of a cockroach, when cornered, it had the ability to fold in on itself and fit into narrow cracks.

The streets were deserted and he and Jas were driving along a main road. Whenever they stopped, the creatures would slowly emerge from the buildings and alleyways to investigate, and they'd learned it paid to keep moving. Bodies were still piled along the sidewalks and on the roads, and the city had taken on an abandoned look, but it was far from empty.

Jas pulled alongside his car and wound down her passenger window. "Where do we stop?"

It was a good question. This had been his city for thirty years, and he wasn't ready to abandon it or its people. Jo had told him he needed to step up and he had, but now he didn't know what to do. They could only fit about eight people in each vehicle, and that assumed they weren't large. Between them, they had enough capacity to move sixteen people per trip, but he wasn't sure where to take them. His idea to stay in the city and help people had been noble, but he suspected it was impractical.

"I dunno. We need to get around sixteen people into the vehicles and outta the city."

"Where are we gonna take them?"

"Anywhere, but here. The city is a death sentence. At least in the country they'll stand a chance."

"Are you sure about that?"

"No, I'm not, but I dunno what else to do."

She was risking her life staying in the city with him, and he guessed she'd signed up to the force for all the right reasons. Like him, she wasn't prepared to walk away and abandon the very people she'd promised to protect. They were slowly cruising past a row of office buildings, when he noticed a frenzy of rapid movement down a narrow alley.

Slowing to a stop, he waited until Jas pulled alongside again and said, "Keep moving. Drive around the block and meet me back here."

"What are you doing?"

"There's something going on down there."

Peering down the alley, dead bodies were lying limp and in impossible positions against the wall, and there was rapid movement in the shadows. The frantic activity was happening in a corner against a dumpster, but all he could see was a blur of black bodies. They formed an angry swarm over something tucked against the large metal bin, and he wound down his window hoping to get a better view. Whatever they were doing, they weren't easily distracted, and he pulled his Glock out of its holster. Using the window frame to hold his arm steady, he pumped three shots into the vibrating throng. The effect was immediate, and they all raised their heads and looked in his direction.

Expecting them to attack, he held his foot over the accelerator, preparing to slam it down and get the hell out of their way. The alleyway was dim, but several of the creatures broke away from the group, and began scuttling over the corpses. Each had twenty long thin legs, and they stopped and hunched over a dead body. While he watched in disgusted fascination, one buried its small oval head into the gut of the rotting corpse. The body was bloated with bluish lines running along the face and exposed arms, and while the creature ferreted inside, it moved as if it was coming back to life. With a seemingly delighted leap, the creature tipped itself up so its rear was in the air, and it began to twitch rapidly.

It was only then he understood what it was doing. It was feeding. The bodies left to rot on the street were their food. While some of the creatures were slowly advancing towards him, a collection of realizations crashed through his numbed mind. Ever since he'd found his wife, Jenny, in their apartment, he hadn't been thinking too cohesively. Surviving from one moment to the next, he'd been moving around in a fog, lacking any real plan and surviving on instinct. Watching the creatures feeding, he now knew they wouldn't kill everyone in the city, and they were intentionally letting some people live. The creatures were demonstrating intelligence. It was as if they had a plan or had done this before. Their once loved city was now a cage, perfectly designed to keep their cattle, and humans were their source of food.

Screwing up his face with contempt and disgust, he opened fire, futilely emptying his rounds into the oncoming creatures. The Glock didn't have enough power to kill them, and he wished he'd used his shotgun.

Jas's car pulled alongside him again and she shouted, "Stop it, Jonesy. We can't deal with them this way."

"You know what they're doing."

"Yeah, I saw enough, but we have to go."

She was right, and he eased his foot against the accelerator, while he pressed the button to raise his window again. He would have left the area, but a woman ran out of a building to his left. She was clutching a small bundle against her chest and waving at him. He hoped she would make it to the car in time, and pressed the button to lower the rear passenger-side window. Seeing his action, the woman suddenly darted forward and threw the bundle into his car. He expected her to follow, but she was whisked away in a blur of black movement. More people were emerging from the building, pushing and dragging children with them. The doors to his car opened and bodies tumbled inside.

"Drive!"

"Go!"

The sudden jumble of movement inside the car caught him by surprise, and he turned to look at their faces. They were young and old, and every single one of them looked terrified. Unable to think of anything to say, he pushed his foot down onto the accelerator, and the car sluggishly began to move.

Jas's car was now behind him, and through his rear vision mirror, he could see she too had a car full of people. Some of the people who'd left the building hadn't made it to their cars, and they were being swarmed by the black creatures. Trying to ignore the scene unfolding behind him, he continued to roll slowly down the road. They couldn't speed down the crowded street and they didn't need to either. He'd already learned, as long as they kept moving, the creatures didn't bother to attack.

Navigating his way along the road, he asked, "Is this everyone in your group?"

"No," A man replied grimly. "There are hundreds of people left in there."

"So, why did only you people leave?"

Through tears, a woman in the back of his car replied, "We saw your cars and argued about who would get to go. They let me go because I'm pregnant."

"Who's they?"

"The others," she replied unhappily. "They sent the kids as well."

He quickly glanced at the man next to him. "Why did they let you go?"

"They didn't," the woman replied bitterly.

The man twisted in his seat to face her with a fierce expression. "It's survival of the fittest now."

He wanted to boot the man out of the car, but stopping would have been more dangerous than letting him stay. "That was an asshole way to behave."

The man gave him a twisted smile and pulled a handgun from his jacket pocket. Waving the gun at him, he said, "Drive and I'll let you know when to get out."

He clearly thought he could steal their vehicle and leave everyone stranded. After everything he'd seen over the past two days, a man with a gun was the least of his worries. Maybe three days ago he would have been alarmed, but now all he felt was offended. A small part of his mind registered he was more outraged by their situation than the man with the gun. The city he'd protected for thirty years had fallen to cockroaches, and this man was willing to kill even more people just to save his own skin. They'd lost everything overnight to something that he should have been able to crush under his shoe. Without thinking, his right arm shot out, and he punched the man in his scowling face. Not content with the one blow, he continued to hammer his thick fist into his face in sharp aggressive bursts. The man's head was slamming against the window, bouncing with each blow.

Through the sound of his fist against the man's face and his painful grunts, he could hear someone laughing behind him. The woman, who only moments earlier had been crying, was now howling with unrestrained delight. Tears were still streaking down her face, only now they were no longer despairing.

In between gasps of giggles, she said, "It's about time somebody punched that jerk."

The man seemed dazed by his repeated blows, and his gun had fallen from his hand and into his lap. Snatching up the weapon, he could already tell from its weight that it was empty.

"Actually, it was kinda stupid. I'm lucky his gun was empty."

A pale hand reached between the two seats. "You're kidding? He's been threatening to shoot anyone and everyone."

"We should kill him," a young girl said angrily.

"Hush, sweetie," the pregnant woman replied. "Don't talk like that."

He'd lost count of how many kids had been pushed into the back of the car, but they complicated his next steps. He could hardly kick them out at the edge of the city as he'd planned.

They'd reached an open parking lot still filled with cars and he stopped. Leaning across the dazed man, he opened the door and said sternly, "This is your stop."

When the man didn't move and continued to look confused, he twisted in his seat and shoved him out of the open door. The man tumbled onto the tarmac, and he leaned across even further to pull the door closed again.

"What happened to him?" Jas asked, once she'd pulled alongside him.

"He pissed me off."

"Now what?"

"What have you got in your car?"

"Two adults and four kids."

Doing a quick headcount, he replied, "I've got one adult and at least five kids here."

"We'll have to take them back to the base."

Driving along the road leading out of the city, he was surprised when another man flagged them down. Seeing he was going into the city rather than out of it, he stopped the car. The man looked to be in his mid-forties, and he was carrying a military-style backpack.

Stopping near the man, he called, "Turn around. The city isn't safe."

The man jogged to his window. "I need to get to University Hospital."

"Why are you going there?"

"I was there with some kids, but the army got us out and took us to Kirtland Air Force Base."

"Why'd you leave the base?"

The man looked down the road towards the city. "It's no safer there than it is in the city. There's no military at the base, only civilians."

"Is that why you left?"

"No, I want to use the equipment at the hospital to analyze the...things."

Since punching out his frustration at the man who'd tried to carjack him, his brain was finally working clearly. "You'll never survive in the city. Come with us, we're heading back to the base."

"There's no point. People are already turning there as well. Believe me, it's not safe there."

"Then where else do you suggest?" Flicking his thumb over his shoulder, he added, "I've got five kids and a pregnant woman in here. Jas has more kids in her car."

The man nodded. "I can see that. I'm a doctor, well, an Oncologist." He was clearly torn about what to do next, and he peered through the passenger window at the children. Sighing, he seemed to make a decision. "A Colonel brought me to the outskirts of the city. He and some other soldiers are heading to Johnsondale in California."

"Why are they going to Johnsondale?"

"There's a secured site there with some tech and weapons they think they can use against these things."

He was growing worried about being parked for too long and asked impatiently, "I thought you said there was no military."

"There isn't. I think the army are running a bit wild, I mean, they're not doing anything bad, but the soldiers I met seemed to be operating independently. I think their command structure has fallen apart."

If the base wasn't safe, then there was no way he was going to dump the kids and pregnant woman there. He didn't want to leave the city, but there was nothing he could do for it. His wife was effectively dead, his home was gone, and his much-loved city was a hellhole.

Warily watching the area through his windshield, he said, "We've gotta keep moving, so you need to make a decision."

The man didn't answer, but walked around the front of his car and opened the passenger side door. Dumping his pack in the well, he climbed into the seat. "I'm Dayton."

"I'm Jonesy. So, where exactly is this safe site in California?"

"They gave me a map. If I found out anything useful, they wanted me to head to a company called CaliTech." Pulling a folded sheet of paper from his pocket, he added, "You need to head west along the I-40."

CHAPTER TWENTY-NINE:
Running blind
(Bill)

With so many people arriving at the base there was no shortage of vehicles, and they'd left in one of the HUMVEEs they'd found parked near the building. The sound of gunfire had followed in their wake, and although he'd wanted to turn around and deal with it, his commonsense had prevailed and they'd kept driving. The base wasn't the safe haven Jo had hoped it would be, and he looked at her stern face while she sat behind the wheel. She couldn't be described as a typically attractive woman. Her body was solidly built, and the lines around her mouth and forehead told him her rank had been hard won. She had a steeliness to her manner and her words, and he doubted any of the men under her command had ever questioned her orders. Despite being told to think otherwise, he couldn't help seeing women as being less able than a man, but he had a suspicion Jo would prove him wrong.

"Do you think the base fell?" He asked.

"Yes," she replied curtly.

Sitting behind him were a man and woman dressed in fatigues, who'd only identified themselves as Curtis and Levy. He didn't know either of them, but as they'd climbed into the truck to leave, the pair had asked to join them. No longer sure of his command, he hadn't asked whether they were really in the military. Pointing out the miles per gallon on the HUMVEE were poor, Jo had said they would need to refuel regularly, and he'd gotten her unspoken message that the extra guns might be useful. No one had spoken much, and he guessed they just wanted to get out of the base before all hell broke loose. The situation really had disintegrated into every man for himself. So far they'd managed to fill the HUMVEE by siphoning gas from abandoned trucks and cars, but now they were getting closer to Johnsondale there were fewer cars on the road.

Continuing to keep an eye out for abandoned vehicles, he mused, "These freaks might have taken over and killed people, but we've still got a lot of equipment. All we need are the troops to use it."

"Are you still going on about the missiles?"

"And helis."

"My precinct had a coupla helis, but we lost contact with them early on," she replied steadily. "I assume they went down, but I never did find out."

"How could they have taken a heli out?"

"Maybe they can fly."

Giving her a quizzical look, he wondered just what their enemy was capable of. Other than the dead one at the mall, all he'd seen were black, rubbery half-human creatures running around like maniacs, and with their rapid movement, it was hard to get a fix on what they else they might be able to do. The doctor had said they were solid, eyeless, and had no discernable organs, which matched his own observations. His experience had proven to him they could only be stopped with a .50-cal weapon or above. They'd obviously started as human, but had evolved into black creatures, and it was feasible they could continue to change.

"Is it a virus?" He asked.

Jo was travelling at thirty miles an hour trying to maximize their gas, and while they drove along the dusty road, it was hard to believe anything was wrong. The side of the road was covered in scrubby bushes, and occasionally he saw cans and other litter. Other than the lack of cars on the road, everything looked pretty much the same as it always had.

"Maybe, but then why are some people immune?" Jo asked in reply.

"Are they immune or have they just not contracted the virus yet?"

She pursed her lips, making her look even more stern than usual. "If it's a virus then how's it transmitted? If it's by air then we should all have it, particularly in the cities. If it's on contact, then why would they be killing people and not infecting them?"

They were good questions and he couldn't answer them. "I don't know. Regardless of how it's transmitted, what's the incubation period?"

Pursing her lips again, she replied, "The insanity appears to be immediate. When we first started getting reports, people thought they were being attacked by other people, not critters. They would have mentioned that in the 911 calls."

"So, they don't fully change immediately. They become lunatics first, and then they turn into black, rubbery critters?"

She nodded. "That stacks up. They said the nav could see them before they turned, so they're giving off a different signal that the visor can read."

"Why would they give off a different signal?"

Shrugging, she replied, "I don't know what the visor reads, but I assume it could be electromagnetic or radiation. If that's the case, then they're not reading as human."

"Or possibly even animal, but that would make them a very different species to anything we've seen before."

"All the more reason not to assume they can't fly. You can't even assume they'll all evolve into the same thing. Maybe there's more than one type."

Giving her an appraising look, he was impressed by her logical thinking. Jo was proving to be more capable than many of the men he'd worked with over the decades. "You're pretty smart."

"You mean for a woman?" She replied, with a slight edge of contempt in her voice.

He was skirting dangerous territory, and turned to stare out of the window at the passing scenery. There was nothing to look at, but he didn't want to get this woman offside. Firstly, he liked her, and secondly, she could use a gun and they needed to work together.

"I could have joined the military," she continued conversationally. "I just figured the police force was smaller and I'd have a better chance of climbing the ranks."

Relieved she hadn't taken deep offence, he replied, "You certainly did that. Commander is a pretty decent rank."

She snorted. "You and I are pretty close to the same rank, Colonel, only there were a lot fewer positions in the police force at my level and even fewer women."

"What's your point?"

"Don't underestimate me like everyone else has in the past and we'll get along fine. I know what you are and the world you were part of. I'll forgive you for being a little...out of touch, but don't be an idiot about it."

The two people behind him, who he now guessed really were in the military, snorted appreciatively at her point. "Yes, ma'am," he replied sheepishly. It seemed to be the only response to such a bluntly made point.

They were entering the outskirts of a small town in Arizona and Jo said sharply, "Look lively, people."

Any delusions he might have held that all was well were quickly lost. Several of the small buildings along the side of the road had clear signs of a gun battle. The glass in the shopfronts had been shot out, and a car had been driven through the wall of a single story building. When he looked closer, he could see some of the abandoned cars had bloody spray against the windows, and he didn't doubt there were bodies inside. It was another lost town, and Jo slowly drove along the road, navigating around the vehicles. One they'd cleared the small town, there was a gas station with a faded diner next to it.

"We need gas," she said firmly, and stopped the HUMVEE fifty yards from the entrance to the station.

While the engine idled loudly, they all peered through the windows looking for any sign of movement. The small forecourt had four old fashioned looking pumps, and the cashier's window was a small booth under a dusty canopy. The sliding window to the booth was open, and he hoped there was still power to the pumps. A tired looking diner sat hunched a short distance from the station, and there were only a few cars parked in front of it. Surrounded by scrubby desert, the whole place had an abandoned feel to it, and given how small the town was, he suspected that was always true, end of the world or not.

"Let's do it," he said decisively.

Jo drove the truck up to the pump furthest from the diner and cashier window. The two troopers immediately climbed out and began to pull the hose towards the gas cap on the truck. One stood guard while the other put the nozzle into the open hole.

"We need to get inside and authorize the pump," Jo said.

He was already outside the vehicle and looking across at the diner. The lack of movement inside bothered him and he peered back into the cab at Jo. "Stay at the wheel."

With his weapon trained on the diner, he walked to the cashier window. Unsurprisingly, there was no one inside, and he reached through the window hoping to find the button that would switch the pumps on. Unlike the computerized counters in the city, it was a simple layout designed for staff with minimal training. Unsure which button would do what, he began to flick different ones. He was rewarded with the sound of the pump coming to life, and he assumed the troopers were filling the tank.

The diner would have supplies and water, and he looked across at it hopefully. The HUMVEE would take at least five minutes to fill, which meant he had some time to kill. With his weapon trained at the wide glass window, he walked across the station towards the diner. It might be empty and it might not be, but he was carrying a M26 shotgun and it could take down any critter or man. With only a five round magazine, it wasn't designed for rapid fire, and he'd need to use his bullets conservatively. Across his other shoulder, he was carrying his M4A1. In his mind, he decided he would deal with human enemies with a regular gun, and would save the M26 for the critters.

Using one of the pumps as cover, he switched to his M4A1, and peered around the edge of the metal box. There was still no movement, and he could hear the heavy hum of the pump continuing to fill their tank. He really should wait with the truck, but after having to run from the bunker, the city and then the base, he was feeling a bit useless. Cutting across the fifty yards from the gas station to the diner was a no-man's land, and he'd be an easy target. He needed to draw out anything that was inside. Firing high into the glass frontage, the window collapsed in on itself with a loud crash. It splintered the silence, and he flinched, now worried he might draw critters to their position.

Jo leaned from the window and called, "What are you doing?"

He didn't need Jo telling him that shooting out a window to get food and water they could live without was a stupid thing to do. They might have only just met, but he could already hear her telling him to act his age and his rank. Not bothering to answer her, he waited to see if there was any response from the diner. When there wasn't, he switched weapons to the M26, and ran forward in a crouch.

Reaching the outside of the diner door, he slammed into the wall next to the entrance. "Is anyone in there?"

To his surprise, a woman's voice replied indignantly, "Why'd ya do that? Now them things can get in."

"How many of you are there?"

"Jus' the two of us. We was doin' fine until ya shot the damn window."

"We need supplies."

"Well, ya coulda just asked like a normal person," the woman replied, sounding increasingly offended.

Standing in the doorway, he finally saw the speaker. She was a short, plump woman, and she had a shotgun trained in his direction. "Who else is here?"

"That ain't none of your business. You army or somethin'?"

"Yes and no."

"That's not an answer."

"Lower your weapon."

"Lower yours first."

He stared over his gun at the woman and she was glaring back at him. Her dry, yellowing blonde hair was pulled into an untidy bun, and she was wearing an apron over her jeans and t-shirt. Clearly she worked at the diner.

"We don't have time for this."

"Where are ya goin'?"

"Johnsondale. There's a company there we need to get to."

The woman lowered her shotgun. "You mean CaliTech."

"Yeah, how do you know about it?"

"I don't, but a lotta people come along this road on their way there. Why are ya goin' there?"

"It's secure and they have some tech we need to deal with the critters."

The woman snorted. "Is that what you're callin' 'em? Critters?"

"Do you know where the site is?"

"Based on what folk told me I know where it is in Johnsondale well enough." The woman gave him a final appraising look and then turned. "Callie, get out here!"

A young woman emerged from the bathroom at the back of the diner. She looked about sixteen and was clearly very frightened. "This is my niece. If CaliTech is safe then I want her to go with ya."

Lowering his weapon, he asked, "What about you? I've only got a rough map to CaliTech, and we could do with some help finding the place."

The woman shrugged. "If you've got the room, then I'll come too." Finally dropping her shotgun to hip level, she added, "I'm Margie."

The HUMVEE was only designed to seat four and it was a tight fit with six people. By the time they'd reached Route 178, they'd passed many small towns that appeared to be abandoned, but it was possible there were people hiding inside the buildings. Occasionally they saw other cars on the road, but no one seemed inclined to stop. He was well aware he had no army behind him, and was effectively just another civilian trying to survive Armageddon. Without the strength of the Army, there wasn't much he could do, and he was rapidly losing confidence and direction. Who was he without his uniform and troops under his command? It was a question he'd never expected to answer until the day he retired.

He was driving and everyone else was asleep or dozing, when he saw a bloodied body lying in the middle of his side of the road. Unwilling to run over the corpse, he slowed the HUMVEE and veered to the middle of the two lanes. Nearing the body, he noticed it was a dark-haired woman with long legs hanging behind her, as if she'd been dragging herself by her arms. The human desire to survive always impressed him. People didn't die willingly, and they would go to extraordinary lengths for even one more day of life. Slowly passing her, he peered out of the driver's window, studying the area behind her feet. Just as he suspected, there were drag marks leading to a car that had obviously crashed into a building by the side of the road. There was another body lying on the hood of the car, and that man was dead too. The woman must have survived the accident, and dragged herself to the road, hoping to find help.

Slowing to a stop, he grabbed his M4A1 and opened the driver's door.

"Where are you going?" Jo asked, opening one eye at him.

"There's a body back there."

Not waiting to hear Jo's answer, he walked back to where the body was lying. The woman was stretched across the road with her heavy hiking boots lying in the dirt, and he could clearly follow the path she'd crawled from the car to the road. Crouching on one knee, he placed two fingers against her neck, feeling for a pulse. Her neck felt warm, and even without finding a heartbeat, he was fairly sure the woman was still alive. Rolling the woman onto her back, he gently patted her cheek, and her eyes fluttered open. There was crusted, brown blood on her dust-covered face, her mouth was split and dry, and she flicked a swollen tongue across her lips.

The woman tried to speak, but all he could hear was a croaking cough. Jo had appeared at his side, and was cautiously watching the road around them. "What are you doing, Bill?"

"She's alive."

Turning to face the HUMVEE, she called, "Curtis! Levy! Give us a hand."

While Jo organized the troopers, he leaned down to the woman's mouth. She was trying to say something, but her voice was no more than a whisper. "Ally."

He didn't understand what she was trying to say. "Is that your name? Ally?"

Her eyes fluttered, and she nodded her head slightly.

He was fed up with feeling out of control and unable to do what he was trained and paid for. If he was honest, he didn't really know what he'd find at CaliTech, but it felt good to be able to help at least one person. Knowing he wasn't being entirely truthful, he said soothingly, "Okay, Ally, hang in there. We're heading somewhere safe. There'll be help for you there."

CHAPTER THIRTY:
New Army
(Leon)

The road leading to the CaliTech site was well concealed, and they would have missed the turn off if Lexie hadn't prodded him sharply in the ribs. The site was over a mile from the main road, along a winding single lane track. The first sign they had of CaliTech was a ten-foot high concrete wall painted a light green to blend in with the trees and grass surrounding it. There was a fifty-yard clearance around the perimeter, and cameras were mounted every fifty yards above the wall. The gates seemed to merge into the wall, and there was no speaker box to contact the people inside, but as they slowly drove up the driveway, the heavy barriers swung open.

The second set of gates were thirty yards from the first, and there was another equally high wall, only this one was painted white. Again, cameras were mounted every fifty yards, and there were black boxes at regular intervals along the wall.

"What are the black boxes for?" Trigger asked.

"Guns," Lexie replied bluntly.

"Is that even legal?" Tuck asked skeptically.

She shrugged. "I dunno, but I guess it doesn't matter if no one knows they're here."

"You're not allowed to shoot people at will," Tuck replied. "Believe me, I've asked and I'm always told no."

Trigger chuckled. "Well, not here anyways."

The second set of gates opened as unbidden as the first, and he assumed they were being watched. It was very tight security, and it made him wonder just how much clout the company had. "Who runs this outfit?"

"Dunk the Skunk...well, he did. I think Ark just took it over," Lexie replied.

"What do you mean?"

"Ark sent him to his office like a naughty boy. Apparently he wasn't being a team player."

"Isn't he the boss?"

Lexie laughed, and he'd noticed the closer they'd gotten to CaliTech the happier she was becoming. She had a pretty laugh and he smiled at her. Her mouth curved into a wide smile of her own and she said, "I don't think anyone's the boss anymore, but I trust Ark, so I'm glad he's in charge."

Once they'd cleared the second set of gates, they were met by a wide expanse of lawn, and a huge four-story building sat in the center of it. Made of steel and painted cream, every window was shuttered with a matching cover, and they blended so well with the walls it was hard to tell where they were. The central doors leading into the building were also closed, and the driver stopped next to the stairs leading to them. He was about to ask how they were going to get inside, when a concealed side door at the top of the short flight of stairs swung open.

A man dressed from top to toe in black stepped outside into the daylight. He was wearing a visor and helmet similar to the one Lexie had worn, and across his shoulders was a heavy looking thick armor that travelled the length of his arms. His hands weren't visible under the boxy gloves, but the barrels from his weapons were. Around his waist was a thick, wide belt filled with large cartridges he assumed were ammo for the guns mounted on his shoulders and along his arms. His legs were built like tree trunks, and starting at his knees was a solid boot that clearly provided even more armor to his lower body. He was over a foot wider than your average man and a foot taller. With the significantly heavier and more complex armor and weapons, Lexie's gear was clearly lightweight by comparison. He assumed he was looking at the type of Navigator they referred to as a tank.

Lexie didn't wait for them and she was already out of the vehicle. She skipped up the stairs, slipping on them as she went. For someone who was so nimble in her armor, she was ridiculously clumsy without it. As he climbed out of the truck, he heard her shriek in delight.

"Tank!"

The enormous Navigator dwarfed her, but somehow managed to bend one stiff looking arm to return her hug.

"Eww, you stink! What have you been playing in?"

Tank flicked his lower helmet up and said blandly, "Critters."

Their squad was emerging from their trucks and slowly making their way up the stairs. Tank stepped aside from the door, and waved a huge arm at them indicating they should go inside. With only his lower face visible, he wasn't sure how to respond to the man, and he obediently walked through the door. Behind the faceless façade of the building was an entirely different world. Bright lights shone down into a huge open area. There were hundreds of workbenches surrounded by boxes, screens and hanging Navigator suits. People were working on the different types of armor and hydraulics, and large screens hung from the ceilings. Music was playing in the background, and there was a rumble of hundreds of voices talking at once. Helmets were propped up on the tables, where people wearing metallic goggles were using fine tools on them. He wasn't sure what he expected to find at CaliTech, and the hub of energy and clearly well-organized activity caught him by surprise.

While he stood slack-jawed and trying to understand what he was looking at, a man rolled forward in an electric wheelchair. Half his face had been burned and large patches of his hair were missing. His jaw was uneven, giving him a twisted mouth, and he suspected it had been reconstructed. It appeared the man was missing his legs from the knees down, and when he checked the man's hands, at least one finger was missing from each. The hands had also been burned, and they had the complex puckered scars consistent with that type of injury. It was obvious the man had been torn apart, and they'd reconstructed him as well as they could.

None of his wounds detracted from the sharp and intelligent eyes that stared back at him from the scarred face. They were a deep and vivid blue, and the unnaturally smooth skin around them crinkled oddly when he smiled. Despite being caught off guard by the man's profound injuries, he found himself smiling back at him.

"Leon," the man said in a steady voice he instantly recognized.

"Ark."

He put his hand out to shake his, but Lexie pushed it aside and threw her arms around Ark. "I've had a horrible time. Don't send me into real combat again."

Ark pulled her into his lap and wheeled himself forward. "I make no promises, Two One. Stop complaining." Looking up at him, he added, "Welcome to CaliTech. Dunk the Skunk liked to keep people onsite for month long shifts, so we have a dormitory here for the workers that you can stay in. We're just getting a full manifest of what we have in inventory. There's training facilities in another building plus a small hospital."

"And a cafeteria," Lexie added, and he guessed she was hungry.

The mention of food reminded him they hadn't had a full meal since before they'd been captured and almost killed. They'd been constantly on the move for six days, and he was beginning to realize just how tired he was under the adrenalin that had kept him going.

Ark nodded. "Dunk's a crazy asshole, and he kept a warehouse full of basic materials, including weapons and food, so we're set up for a while at least."

Following Ark, they all began to walk the length of the building. Donna had already disappeared, but he supposed for her and Lexie this was their home. Lexie had bounded from Ark's lap, and he guessed she'd gone wherever Donna had. No one was paying much attention to the dirty, well-armed soldiers walking across their production floor, and they didn't seem surprised to see them. Ark was explaining what they were doing on the workbenches, but he wasn't really listening. He looked across at Tank who was walking next to him. In response, Tank turned his head so he could see his own face in the visor covering his eyes.

"What's the plan, Tank?"

Tank snorted softly, but didn't reply. Ark looked up at him and said, "We need nav boots out there, so you're gonna get some training."

He glanced at Tuck who looked back at him with his mouth set in a fixed grim line. Shaking his head, he said bluntly, "I don't wanna be blinded like Lexie."

With a loud creaking, Tank lifted his heavily armored hands to his head and pulled his helmet off. To his surprise, the visor came away with the helmet and Tank looked at him coolly. "We're not all blind. The orbs are only needed for advanced vision."

Ark chuckled. "So, what do ya reckon? Think you want some training?"

For the first time since he'd almost had his head cut off, he grinned widely. "So, what kinda weapons have you guys got?"

Rolling his chair forward, Ark gave a flamboyant wave of his scarred hand. "Let me show you our armory." Suddenly he stopped rolling and seemed to be listening intently to his earpiece. After a short pause, he said sharply, "On my way."

Turning his chair abruptly, he began to roll towards a set of elevators tucked away against the far wall of the vast production floor.

Picking up on his shift in mood, he asked, "What's wrong?"

"The missiles are flying," Ark called over his shoulder.

"What does that mean?"

Ark was already well ahead of them and Tank replied grimly, "They're bombing the cities."

"Why? The critters are in the desert."

"They probably don't know that."

If they were bombing their own cities, then NORAD must believe the entire country had fallen. Worse still, they didn't even know their enemy was forming camps, and they were targeting the wrong places. Destroying their own cities was an act of desperation, and he worried even more about Amelia. What if they'd bombed Seattle?

Ark had already reached the elevators and was waiting for them to catch up. As he walked towards him, he studied the profoundly injured man thoughtfully. His wife and unborn son were probably already dead, there was no military left, the cities had fallen, and no one could be trusted anymore. If they were going to survive, they'd have to learn to fight an enemy they'd never planned for. The Navigator technology might give them an edge they couldn't get any other way, and clearly Ark was already thinking about how they could take back control. He was quite possibly the only person who had a plan for their survival that had any chance of success.

Standing in the elevator next to Ark, he leaned down and said firmly, "Okay. Let's kick some alien ass."

EPILOGUE
(Steve)

He was feeding in a thousand parts and satisfying the hunger that had been growing inside him. Buried deep under the earth, he leaned back into the sticky mud and sucked at the wall, drawing moisture into his body.

This was the cycle. Seeding the colony was only the first step. Birth was followed by food. Food was followed by colonization. Colonization was followed by domination. Domination was followed by exploration, and the cycle would begin again. It was a perfect cycle.

He wasn't alone. He was never alone. There were more minds just like his, with millions of creatures under their control, and he knew they were feeding just as he was.

Also by SD Tanner
Books in *Hunter Wars* Series

(Series One of The Hunter Wars)

Book One:
EVE OF THE HUNTER WARS

Book Two:
HEAVEN MEETS HELL

Book Three:
ARMY OF ANGELS

Book Four:
GIFT FROM GOD

Book Five:
RIGHT TO RULE

Book Six:
CALL TO WAR

Books in *Eden Lost* Series

(Series Two of The Hunter Wars)

Book One:
HIDDEN EVIL

Book Two
DEAD ALIVE

Book Three
BATTLEFRONT
(Release: 2016)

Book Four
DIVINE DEATH
(Release: To be scheduled)

Books in *The Locke Files* Series

Book One:
TIME TO DIE

Book Two
TIME TO KILL
(Release: To be scheduled)

Books in *NAVIGATOR* Series

Book One:
ENEMY LINES

Book Two
BLIND SIGHTED

Book Three
KILLER EDGE

Book Four
BROKEN ARROW

Also by SD Tanner
Books in *Hunter Wars* Series

(Series One of The Hunter Wars)

Book One:
EVE OF THE HUNTER WARS

Gears, Pax and TL are brothers and soldiers in the US Army when the world comes to an abrupt halt. Thrust into the apocalypse, they decide mankind deserves another chance. Their ruling puts them at the center of an epic battle between good and evil, and they uncover the hidden truth behind the Devil in the land of the undead. Along the way, they meet a woman they name Ip and their true role is revealed.

Forming the first of their bases, they call survivors to their side and unwittingly make enemies of the undead and the living. Determined to succeed, they take drastic steps to secure safe havens for those left alive.

Book Two:
HEAVEN MEETS HELL

New friends are found, but the face of evil makes its presence known in the safety of their bases. Pax makes a mistake and Ip pays the price, but Gears refuses to let his new enemy rule the day.

Book Three:
ARMY OF ANGELS

Determined to fight fire with fire, Gears offers the survivors the choice of infection. Mackenzie does the unthinkable creating a remarkable outcome that makes Gears question everything he knows about life.

Book Four:
GIFT FROM GOD

Desperate to find safe land where they can grow food, they take the drastic step of seeking safer shores. The Devil takes Pax to a place he never knew existed and Ip learns who she really is. Captain Ted makes a mistake that Gears must undo or they'll lose everything they've gained.

Book Five:
RIGHT TO RULE

Fed up with the Devil's play, Gears is determined to enforce his right to rule. The Devil disagrees and does something they didn't expect, setting them back again. Captain Ted is forced to make a terrible choice and they stand to lose more than they gain. The land is dying and hunger grips their world.

Book Six:
CALL TO WAR

Gears witnesses the impossible and they learn there's more that the Devil can do. Faced with disaster, he calls the game to an end and prepares for a final battle. Mankind must make their true intent known or all will be lost for a thousand years.

Books in *Eden Lost* Series

(Series Two of The Hunter Wars)

Book One:
HIDDEN EVIL

It's been five years since they put the Devil in his place, but all is not well in Eden and our Horsemen have dug their way out of their graves. It seems the Devil wasn't done and neither were they. Gears must uncover his new mission, and he believes he needs another army to defend his right to rule. America is at war with itself and he needs to know why.

Book Two
DEAD ALIVE

The hunters have returned, but they're not the same as they were. Gears, Pax and TL decide they need to look for the problem in Eden and uncover more than they ever expected. Ruler is playing them all for fools, and Gears finds a unique solution to save America.

Book Three
BATTLEFRONT
(Release: Scheduled 2016)

Book Four
DIVINE DEATH
(Release: To be scheduled)

Books in *The Locke Files* Series

Book One:
TIME TO DIE

Jack Locke was an Army Intelligence expert and a criminal investigator. In 2050, scientists learn how to extend life by five hundred years, but the technology also opens the way for race-based genocide and genetic engineering.

Struggling to deal with his tragic past, he finds himself trying to stop the President from using DNA-based biological warfare to cull an over populated world. Locke must protect the world from a technology that aimed to help, but could change what makes us human.

Book Two
TIME TO KILL
(Release: To be scheduled)

Books in *NAVIGATOR* Series

Book One:
ENEMY LINES

After nearly being executed in a war zone, Staff Sergeant Leon Shield finds himself urgently recalled from deployment, and lands back home to a defeated country. In a matter of days, and without a single shot being fired, a new species has taken over the world. Determined to survive Armageddon, the only chance to fight back is to find a man called Ark, and use an untested technology to become Navigators.

With hydraulics, armor and advanced vision, Navigators are soldiers of the future, and in the game of survival of the fittest, they become the only hope man has to fight for their right to dominate.

Book Two
BLIND SIGHTED

Leon and Ark elect to train their new Navigator squad outside the wire, while Bill works with the weapons engineers to solve the bigger problems. The medical team are taking the critters apart, desperately looking for anything that will give them an edge.

Book Three
KILLER EDGE

Our team match the enemy by creating a little critter magic of their own. New forces join them, and survivors add their weight to the fight, further changing what becomes possible. First contact is made, and believing they are running headlong into failure, Ark learns to take the lesser loss.

Book Four
BROKEN ARROW

The aliens take a step too far and Ark decides it's time to go all in. Sending all of their Navigator battle teams to the nests, they uncover unexpected allies in a final showdown that will determine which side will rule earth.

Visit the website at www.sdtanner.com for news, updates and announcements

Follow on Twitter @sdtanner1

Made in the USA
Lexington, KY
30 August 2016